The Common Man

P.L. Howd

Copyright © 2024 P.L. Howd
All rights reserved
First Edition

PAGE PUBLISHING
Conneaut Lake, PA

First originally published by Page Publishing 2024

ISBN 979-8-89315-634-8 (pbk)
ISBN 979-8-89315-647-8 (digital)

Printed in the United States of America

CHAPTER 1

This is a story of an extraordinary man—a man like most others in the sense that he lived an exhausting life and survived an exhausting journey. His name is Sean O'Neill. Most humans will only hear stories about people like Sean because they are so caught up in their own lives, and they are not aware that some people have developed into larger-than-life people. To get to know Sean, we have to go back all the way back to the very beginning so that you can understand what makes a man like Sean so special, so unusual.

In every galaxy, there exists the Creator, an all-knowing and powerful being whose purpose is to create life. During the course of every hour, the Creator generates a cascading waterfall of approximately eight hundred billion new thoughts. Each one of those new thoughts is an individual creation or some sort of life form, such as an animal or an organic creation like a tree.

These thoughts are gathered by tiny servants of the Creator, each of which is designed to take care of its own life form, and every designation of life form has its own caretaker. The Creator of the Milky Way galaxy has set aside a very special task, a task that is reserved for only the very best servants; these servants are his personal gatherers for the most important of all tasks, the task of gathering the thoughts that will be cultivated into human souls. The Creator calls the servants Milkies—not because he's the Creator of the Milky Way galaxy, but because of their translucent appearance. The Milkies all have numeric markings, which distinguish them from other servants. All the other servants can see these marking on Milkies' heads, which distinguish them even more clearly as the ones carrying the most precious thoughts. The other servants stay busy collecting their cargo but keep a wide space open for any Milky. No servant would slow down a Milky who is carrying the Creator's most valuable thoughts. These thoughts are carefully nurtured, cultivated into what will become human souls, the very souls that drive humans to prosper and seek their way in the world.

The Creator has devised a sorting table in which all his thoughts for the day are deposited throughout his Creation. The sorting table can be described in human terms. Picture yourself as the size of a gnat…a tiny insect. Now picture yourself on the edge of a football field. Now you can visualize the size of the sorting table, the one and only means by which each creation travels to earth. Continue visualizing that giant field, through which everything that enters goes straight to earth. Three sides have giant walls or barriers to ensure that every creation makes its way to earth by allowing everything to go into it. In the middle of the sorting table are two special port holes to earth. On what would be the forty yard line on the right side would be a floating upside-down construction cone, about the size of a fifty-five gallon drum standing about four feet tall called the (Eye-EEE). (Remember you're still the size of a gnat.) This is the port hole for the thoughts that will become souls that will be born middle class.

On the opposing forty yard line would be another floating cone known as Mount Soul, however, this one would be approximately ten feet tall, extremely steep sided, with an opening at the top size of a soda can. This port hole is for the souls that are born as czars or emperors. The rest of the sorting table is for the souls that will be born as the common man. This entire area is known as the (Oh-Well).

The Milkies take the thought from the Creator and bring it to the edge of the sorting table. Here they clean it and handle it over and over. Each touch develops the thought, and when the Milky feels that its precious cargo is ready, it brings the thought to the edge of the sorting table, grabs it by the tail, and flings it into the sorting table.

All the thoughts of the Creator enter earth through the sorting table. The only exceptions are the souls that make it into the two floating port hole.

The edge of the sorting table itself is a spacious area in which the Milkies can set down the thoughts from the Creator and prepare them for their journey to earth. Every human soul will find its way to earth, but there are only three portholes.

At this point of soul development, human souls are divided into four groups. The first of which is the hardest to become. These souls must pass through Mount Soul. Most Milkies don't even try to deposit their souls there, as it is a one in one hundred billion chance of making it through, the kind of chance that most souls cannot understand. Most Milkies, because of difficulty, don't even attempt it. It would be like climbing to the top of Mount Kilimanjaro and then finding out you still have to climb the Empire State building by using the stairs, and two out of three stairs are missing.

The Eye-EEE porthole is nearly as difficult. With approximately a one in ten million chance of a Milky depositing its designated soul into it, this is the porthole that most Milkies aim for. It also is like climbing Mount Kilimanjaro, seemingly difficult but not impossible, which is why so many Milkies try for this goal.

The last porthole, the remainder of the table known as the Oh-Well, is the one that gathers all the rest of the souls that will never make the grade of the first two portholes; so it becomes the porthole where all the rest of the servants carry all the other thoughts that are made by the Creator. This is also the porthole that all the other thoughts are sent through to get to earth: the trees, the bushes, the ants and the wasps, the smallest amoebas, and the largest mammals all share this busy porthole.

There is a very small percent of human thoughts that don't quite go in to one of these three portholes smoothly. These are the thoughts that will always try to be different, be outspoken, or give of themselves to benefit another. These thoughts are the ones that will be followed their entire lives from birth to death; they are simply known as the Jumpers! These are the human souls that, as they slung into the sorting table, make contact with either one of the cones. If the souls make contact with either cone long enough, it will give them drive to be more than a common man; therefore, they become Jumpers in their lifetime. Depending on how long they stay connected to the cone before they fall off will determine the strength of their drive to do better in life. The ones that stay on the cone for a long time will end up having a Milky guiding them throughout their life.

You're probably thinking to yourself that a human soul seems to start out like an arcade game of chance, but the creation of a human soul is so much more.

Thoughts are sent to the edge of the sorting table by the servants of the Creator. Human thoughts, when they first appear, look like tiny raindrops with four claws and a tail. The Milkies must gather them as soon as possible for their trip. Each thought that will be developed into a human soul is gathered by its tail by a Milky, since the Milkies are designed differently than any other servant of the Creator. Most of the other servants would be considered to be gnats in comparison to the Milkies, who are like the Clydesdales of servants, with their bumblebee-like bodies.

Gathering the human thoughts of the Creator is just the first step in transferring each future soul to the sorting table. Each time a soul is moved, it develops a little more. The sorting table exists as a cloudy, horizontal doorway for each thought to travel safely to earth to be inserted into the first breath of a human. The doorway to the table is open to all gatherers of all other collectors, making this a very busy gateway. In human terms, the gateway is like a coliseum. It is a vast dark void with two protruding towering cones in the center with the rest wide open. Each porthole, including the main dark void, contains the fate and "destiny of each human soul." Not all Milkies are equal, and that is why most souls are just flung into the dark void. Should a Milky try and fling a soul into one of the cones and miss, it always has a place to go, the large vast opening in the sorting table known as the Oh-Well, because that is what the Milkies shout when they try for a better life for their soul they are flinging when it goes into the black void of the large sorting area. Everybody has their own name for the human souls that get sorted into the Oh-Well, calling them grunts, workers, or commoners. These all mean the same thing, as they are the humans that'll have to work their whole existence and then die in the same conditions in which they were brought into this world. I call these people the Common Man. Your status has no bearing on whether you are a man or woman, your race or your religion, how big or how small you are, right-handed or left-handed. It all comes down to the fact that you were put into the Oh-Well sorting area, and then down the funnel you went.

Regardless of where the soul enters the porthole, they will all find their way to a new human who is being born, and upon the babies taking their first breaths, souls are inserted, giving the humans drive, their reason for doing or not doing, what they want to do in life. This is the purpose of their soul, that little itch in your brain that says, should I do this, or should I not do this? The right or wrong, the good or the bad, and the will to live.

The funnel to the right side of the launching area is much harder for the Milkies to flick the new souls into. It sits much higher, with steeper outside walls worn fairly smooth. A small portion of human souls are still able to be flicked into this porthole with a much smaller hole on the top, and this one has become known as Eye-EEE, again because that's the sound that the Milkies make when a soul goes in.

With so many Milkies flicking so many souls throughout the day, there are still a great number of souls that make it into the Eye-EEE funnel. These are the humans that are labeled as nobles and chiefs, religious and political leaders. The commoners call these people the middle or upper class. These human souls will live a life of means that commoners aspire to achieve with a much more comfortable and enjoyable life.

The left side of the launching area is a smooth funnel, eight times higher with Milky Guards positioned all around the top to prevent any ordinary souls from clawing themselves anywhere near the top. It also has a wandering air current that most souls can't get past. Sometimes it can be decades or tens of decades before even a single soul can get flicked into this hole by a Milky. At times, it has been years before even one soul has challenged a guard. To most Milkies, this funnel is a mystery, as mysterious as the Loch Ness monster, as elusive as Bigfoot, and as rare as a UFO to humans. Milkies are not allowed to fly over the top of this porthole so that there is not a chance of a soul accidently falling into it. This porthole is only known as Mount Soul because only rare souls ever touch it. If a soul would manage to get inside and descend through this porthole, they would become a czar or an emperor, a supreme ruler in an area. These are the humans that go down in history as the most powerful humans. History remembers these people because of their strengths or the ruthlessness, their kindness or their cruelness. These humans' names are engraved on the inside of Mount Soul so that as any other soul that enters this porthole will know the powerful and great rulers that have graced the earth over the eons, and as the new soul goes by, its name will be engraved in Mount Soul.

This all sounds simple enough, but there is always a glitch in everything, and so there is a special Council for Milkies that deal with the glitch category. When humans develop, the ones that are always in trouble in life are almost always from the group called the Jumpers. The human soul can be so persistent that most of these humans go crazy trying to achieve what they sense they should have. Jumpers are usually society's problem children, the ones with that desire to do something deep in their soul but with no way or direction to achieve it. The length of time that their souls came in contact with the other portholes will give them the depth of their drive. This is where the Council of Milkies comes into their lives. It is entirely up to the Council to evaluate whether or not the Jumper will advance and do better in life or be subject to a life of never achieving their dreams.

CHAPTER

2

Sean's journey started back in 1964, just another peaceful day for our Creator. A day in time that would start out like most others, it was full of busy collectors, trying to sort another day of the Creator's thoughts. The Milkies were working very hard collecting thoughts. There were so many different varieties of collectors; some were collecting thoughts that would become new species of plants. Other collectors were collecting thoughts that would eat food off of those new plants. All the Creator's servants knew what to do. The Milkies quickly grabbed their assigned thoughts by their tails and then brought them over to the sorting table. The Milkies would take the Creator's thoughts, clean them, shine them, and name them. After being cleaned, shined, and labeled, the thoughts, the size of a grain of sand, were transformed into souls, which would be set on the edge of the table and then flicked onto the sorting area. The majority of the Milkies all tried for at least one of the funnels in the middle of the field, which is why there are so many more humans around the center of the earth than on the poles of earth. The sorting table not only sorts human souls into social classes, but also sends every thought geographically to be distributed throughout the earth; each location on the sorting table corresponds to a location on earth. The location closest to center of the sorting table will deliver straight to the center of the equator. Each Milky took great pride shining, polishing, and developing each thought, then trying to get a human soul into one of the special cones. Depending on how many times each soul was handled by its Milky will depend on the size and shape of each soul. This is the main reason that each soul is flung into a different spot. Each soul is different, even just a little; one may have been handled more than the next or shined more than others. This is one of the reasons why humans, even with similar DNA, develop differently. Between the Milkies and all the other servants flinging their creations into the table, it is one of the busiest places in the Milky Way.

The sorting table is always full of activity, with a plethora of different creations consistently going into the Oh-Well, one after another, and several of the souls smacking into the sides of the two protruding funnels. If a human soul makes contact, they are quickly identified as a Jumper, and the Milky that flung that soul would follow that soul down the Oh-Well to oversee that human as it develops. The longer the souls stay in contact with the cone, the stronger they will be as a Jumper.

This day would be different; this day would be a day Milkies rarely got to see in their lifetime. Milky number MV-2 took aim and flung a soul that it had labeled Paul, hitting the top of Mount Soul.

A tremendous roar let out from the top of Mount Soul!

This sound caught the attention of each and every Milky Guard that was guarding the entry of the Mount Soul porthole. All the guards turned around and headed up to the top to try to remove the possible Jumper. Paul held onto the top of the funnel, instinctively trying hard to climb inside. Paul heard the thunder of the Milky Guards trying to close in on him. The top of the porthole was shaking with high winds and the thundering of the guards. These particular Milky Guards were created solely for one purpose—to remove the Jumpers. They were positioned on each of the portholes with sharp claws to aid them on climbing on the portholes, allowing them to dig in and not fall off. Each claw on a guard's feet produced a light show as their claws dug into the portholes with energy similar to static electricity. The guards' only job was to remove anything on the sides of their portholes, and they did their job well.

Paul could now feel the energy of power coming from the guards and the energy from inside the porthole as well.

Almost there! The side was too slick for Paul's little claws to hold onto. He pulled with all his might and looked inside. Almost in, Paul held on tight, still reaching over the ledge.

Just then, another Milky took aim, flinging a soul named Sean, ricocheting off the Milky Guard that was near Paul and landing square on Paul's back. Down the side of the porthole went the guard. Sean held onto the back of Paul, while Paul was holding on for all he could on the top of Mount Soul.

Normally if a soul comes in contact with another soul, one or both of the souls die, and the humans that receive those souls are born as a still born. Somehow, neither of the souls died. Sean clawed onto Paul's back, pinning him to the top edge. Then, looking into the top of Mount Soul, Sean was so amazed at the sight that he stopped. Sean held onto Paul, trying to get himself over the top and into Mount Soul. For a moment, Sean stopped struggling, because he thought he was seeing through eyes that weren't his. Both Paul and Sean were on the top edge of the Mount Soul, both pulling, struggling, trying to get into the top, while more souls were flinging by. One by one, the other souls would all fall into the darkness of the Oh-Well. Down and out of sight they went.

Sean was determined not to fall into the Oh-Well. All of a sudden, he felt the electricity from a Milky Guard grab him. Sean could feel his tail absorbing the electricity, paralyzing it into a stiff rod. Then he could not hold on anymore. The Milky Guard flung Sean off the side and down into the darkness of the Oh-Well. Paul was so busy watching Sean's departure into the darkness that another Milky Guard came up, grabbed him, and also flung him as well, down into the darkness of the Oh-Well. The Milky Guards talked among themselves, amazed that both souls survived contact. The Milkies were so busy talking that they did not accompany their Jumpers through the Oh-Well. Both souls, now Jumpers, were now unaccompanied!

Number MV-2 huddled up with all the other Milky collectors who witnessed what had just happened. Number ME-521 and ME-933 said, "Did you see that soul grab hold of the one that was going into the top?"

Another Milky said, "The Council is not going to like this not one bit."

Milky number MV-2 knew he had to report to the Council that there was a situation, a situation that was normally just dismissed.

This was different. Number MV-2 knew this was different; neither of the Jumpers died from contacting each other. They both survived!

"This was different, but how do I explain what I saw?" said MV-2.

ME-933 said, "Do you think that either of the Jumpers saw inside of Mount Soul?"

MV-2 responded, "I don't know, but there is something different about that soul, Sean. He held onto that other Jumper. We are going to have to report this."

The group of Milkies flew off to the report to the council.

The Council was a group of beings that enforced the Creator's guidelines and decisions for human development. They are the Creator's police, human advocates, prosecutors, and executors on all things that pertain to humans.

The Council gathered in a chamber that looked like a snow crystal, a crystal lined maze with tens of thousands of windows for the Council to view the activity on earth. MV-2 went to the Council chambers and went in.

Oden, the second most powerful of the council members, approached MV-2 at the gate.

Oden listened to the story, and after MV-2 finished, he was told to wait outside while Oden called the other members of the Council for a meeting. After a short time, Oden came out and told MV-2 to wait at the edge of the sorting table for further direction.

While MV-2 waited on the edge, thirty other Milkies were also ordered to the edge of the sorting table and asked to wait on instructions. As they waited, watching the busy activities of the sorting table, Oden approached them.

"With the direction of the Council of Milkies, you are all being sent on a mission of observation and guidance for both of these Jumpers until they are old enough to be tested. They both have the survival gene since they both survived contact," Oden said. "This Sean soul will certainly become a powerful Jumper, but only time will tell what kind of human he will become. He needs to be found and followed. For a human soul to have been able to hold on to another soul is unheard of and could be trouble in his human life.

You all need to follow both of these humans, Sean and Paul, and report to me about the humans as they are trying to develop. That is all."

The entire group was sent down into the sorting table to find the two souls known only as Sean and Paul. MV-2 thought he was prepared for what he faced, but as they all fell through the abyss of the large sorting table, they found themselves being spread out and sorted out farther by quadrants and scattered among the earth. They watched the other souls going through the journey from sorting table to their awaiting human body and watched as the new souls were inserted into the newborn children.

Have you ever wondered the real reason why you have to spank a baby when they are first born? Doctors will tell you it's to make them take their first breath, but it's from the long practice of inserting the human soul.

That human's very first breath!

The first time a baby opens its mouth and inhales that first breath is how the new soul enters. It's like watching the newborn turn on like a light bulb. This is the most miraculous transformation of human development to be observed. It's like an entire city of humans all standing in their doorways, waiting for the power company to turn the power on at the same time. That entire city is the human brain, and at that point, that very millisecond upon the soul entering the brain, is the most magical millisecond of a human's life.

As the Milkies arrived on the earth's surface, they watched their own bodies morph and change into adult humans. They watched their wings fall off, and then they started to stretch to human size. Their skin began to be covered with garments according to the geographical location of where they were.

MV-2 was trying to figure where he was and how to use this human body, when he looked around and thought to himself, *Jungle, definitely in the jungle*. MV-2 came to rest in Central America with a new body and the name of Terrel Brown. Another Milky came to rest near him, taking the name of Clinton Black. Together, Terrel and Clinton spent the next several hours trying to figure out how to use their new bodies.

Terrel told Clinton, "Sure wish we still had our wings! Where do you think we are?"

Clinton said, "As hot as it is, with this many trees, I think we're in the woods in the middle of the earth somewhere. Where do you think we are? Ouch! That bug just bit me! That hurt! This body sucks. If these little bugs hurt this much, then what if something bigger bites me? I am going to be terminated before this journey even begins. Are you being torn up by these little monsters?"

Clinton rambled on as he was practicing walking. "Son of a bitch!" Clinton burst out. "Now the plants are attacking me!" Clinton had gotten too close to some stinging nettles and had that to deal with that also. Terrel chuckled and thought to himself, *Thanks, Oden. I hope the rest of the team isn't as lost in the jungle as we are.*

None of the other Milkies were sorted out in the same area. Oden had told the entire team that when they arrived on earth, they would be able to sense each other's presence, that their number would be a marking behind their ear, that they would receive a human name, and that their last name or surname would be a color to help them locate each other more easily.

Terrel and Clinton did not feel the presence of any other team members, so they knew they were alone in the jungle. However, they also knew that they had several years to find Paul and Sean, since they had just been born today.

Terrel was all about the mission. He was taking this very seriously because he was the one who had flung Sean into the sorting table. Terrel looked around, listening to Clinton's complaining, and that distracted his thinking. Clinton was scratching his now festering legs from the nettles. Terrel stared at him, thinking he had a moron for help. Terrel was focused on finding a direction to go; his mind was going in twelve directions at the same time but still constantly being distracted by Clinton.

Terrel said, "Clinton, the sooner we find Sean, the sooner we become immortal again." Clinton was being bit up by bugs; he seemed to ignore Terrel.

"Clinton! Pay attention. Unless you want to spend the rest of your miserable human existence being eaten up by bugs, we need to come up with a direction to go."

"Okay, we know that Sean was just born, so we have plenty of time to find him and do whatever it takes to make sure that we control this Jumper."

Terrel knew that at least once a year, everyone would have to make contact with the Council and give an update. He thought to himself, *Sure hope he's not in this jungle, because Clinton is going to make this year very uncomfortable.*

Terrel said aloud, "And now the quest begins. Let's go, Clinton! Time to get started."

CHAPTER

3

Sean's parents were Mary and Jeffrey O'Neill, who lived in a modest house in Georgetown, Pennsylvania. Georgetown was a small heavily wooded town on the border of New York and Pennsylvania.

Sean was born into this world as a happy and strong 7.6-pound baby boy with two older sisters. Mary and Jeff were "typical common humans." Mary was a cashier at the corner store, the only job she had ever known, and adored living in the country.

Jeffrey was a carpenter and worked sixty hours a week. His sole passion in life had always been his family, and he never really cared about anything else. Sean's oldest sister was Susan, six years old, with a very athletic ability and beautiful red hair. Susan was not very happy to have a baby brother or, for that matter, not happy to have any siblings at all. Sean's other sister was Luna; Luna was four years old and a spitting image of her mother at this age, with beautiful brunette hair and brown eyes. Luna was very excited to have a baby brother; to Susan, this was the perfect opportunity to play dress-up with somebody, and she seemed to have the built-in instinct for affection and a strong nurturing nature.

Now there was Sean, with bright red hair just like Susan, seeming to be just like any other child, except, unbeknownst to him, his every move and everybody he interacted with would be under careful scrutiny by onlookers.

When Sean was six years old, the first of the Milkies found him. The first to make contact with Sean was a Milky named Mark Goldman. Mark was honored enough to take lead as first finder and injected himself into Sean's life as the swim coach at the Time Management Park, knowing that everybody loves to swim. Here,

Mark felt that he could oversee who Sean was interacting with and watch his development while staying undetected by Sean. By the time Sean was eleven, two more Milkies had found their way into his life.

The second to find Sean was Martha Ruby. Martha, with the direction of Mark, was appointed as school principal at Georgetown School.

The third to find his way to Sean was James White. James found his way at nearly the same time as Martha. James wanted to be the team leader, and he was not happy being the third in line.

James was one of the many Milkies that was damaged upon his entry on earth. James had a wild vine absorb onto him as he was forming upon landing. That vine restricted his development; this made him blind with jealousy. James was the guy that screamed, "See me!" Mark directed James to take a position at the school as the janitor and to observe Sean and his surroundings until further notice. James didn't want anything to do with a support role or doing his job as an overseer. James was what someone would describe as damaged goods. James wanted a leadership role and even though he was damaged goods. He was still a Milky with Milky powers.

James decided that one of the major powers in the area was the sheriff. He set out on his own to take up a position as the Georgetown sheriff. Using his Milky powers of mental telepathy, he forced his way into the community and forced himself into the position as the Georgetown sheriff. Under most circumstances, you would think that James would not have much of a chance due to his appearance and stature. James was average or below average on every account. He was short and stumpy and nearly bald, but the thing that stuck out most about James was that the food that he enjoyed eating would produce a foul body odor (a reaction to the wild vine). James's body shape and smell was definitely a result of the wild vine. For that reason, Mark had assigned him as school janitor where James could observe Sean as he was growing up.

Mark had been given an incredible physique, standing at six feet and three inches with dark skin, steel gray eyes, with an aged look of about forty, and he could swim like a fish. You would've thought he was an Olympic swimmer.

Martha had been given a slightly older body, slim and striking with dark green eyes, and this was the reason that Mark gave her the position as school principal. She really looked the part.

Mark knew that of the thirty overseers assigned to find Sean and Paul, three had found Sean, but how many had found Paul? When would the others arrive? Days passed, and days turned into months, and still it was just Mark and Martha watching over Sean. James remained absent from the position that Mark assigned for him for nearly a year. Martha had felt the presence of James passing by the school many times over the months. Week to week and month by month, he was becoming less and less noticeable as James. Martha was very observant; she sensed James's presence in the area but also sensed that something was very different.

James's scent was not the same as a normal Milky, having instead a rotten scent, and as time passed, his scent as a Milky had diminished to the point that it was nearly undetectable. When Martha would sense James near the school, she knew it was James, because he stunk, like old rotten food, not the distinctive scent of a Milky. When Martha got close enough to him, she saw the unmistakable mark of a Milky, "M1113," showing on the back of James's right ear. Stench and all, it was definitely James. Martha had no idea why James was so different but knew that there was something really off about James. Over time, Martha would follow James around, cautiously waiting for the right time. There was something odd about this Milky that she had not encountered before; it was as if he were more human than a Milky. Maybe, somehow, when James came through the porthole, maybe he got screwed up somehow, maybe his mind got overcooked upon reentry. She wanted to go to see Mark, but she was filled with a sense of duty to Sean and wasn't going to leave the school unattended.

Little did Martha know that James was doing the same thing: following Martha. Over the past year, James has nearly lost his abilities as a Milky because of his inability to operate as a Milky. James had been following Martha because he wanted to take out any and all Milkies that had already come in contact with Sean so he could have lead position. James somehow became a hunter or predator as opposed to being a guardian.

Several weeks passed, and James approached Martha. "Martha, you need to pick a side. I should be lead in charge, not Mark."

Martha replied curtly, "Mark is a good guardian and has bonded well with Sean. You don't even want to take your part as a guardian."

This did not sit well with James, but he knew the laws. James walked away and tried to come up with a plan. "Play nice," he told himself. "I think the boy is old enough to be administered a HEART test." (A HEART test stands for Human Early Advancement Realignment Testing.) This was the only way to test the boy and maybe get rid of Mark. He had to come up with a plan to make the HEART test Mark's idea.

"I think we need to have a meeting with Mark and try to see what this boy can do," he told Martha. "Test him, you know…see what he can do."

Martha was in complete disagreement with this. With a defiant huff, she responded, "He's not yet old enough. I'll fight for this not to happen." She turned and walked away. Martha knew that James would be trouble. It seemed as if he were more interested in ending the possibilities for Sean to become a Jumper from a common man to a noble. Martha had to think. *How can I stop James from getting permission to administer a HEART test on such a young human?*

There was something else that James didn't know—if Sean was proven to be a non-Jumper and just a regular common boy, then all the Milkies who were assigned as guards would spend the rest of Sean's life running interference on him, assuring that Sean would never become a noble and that he would spend the rest of his life as a common man.

Martha stewed about it all night and in the morning went down to Time Management to speak to Mark. As she arrived at Time Management, Martha could feel the presence of something stronger than one Milky. *I can't believe that James beat me down here*, she thought.

James managed to persuade Mark even though James had been nothing but defiant in the observation of Sean. Mark decided that he could devise a HEART test to see if Sean was a Jumper.

"I've seen nothing to indicate that Sean is ready to be a Jumper," Martha said.

"We shall see. It's not just about being a Jumper. This boy could be the one, the one who exposes the order of the sorting table and how to change the human destiny," Mark replied. According to Oden, there is so much more at stake here.

Martha blurted out, "He's just a boy." Mark put his head down and started to walk away.

"I will arrange for a HEART test…very soon at the pool."

Martha, still resistant, said, "There has never been a HEART test on a human so young. Do you really think this could be the one?"

Mark said, "Sean O'Neill is going to have a day that he will never forget."

Mark spent the whole night tossing and turning. He was accustomed to giving tasks and challenges, but this was going to be different. Sean was only twelve years old, and most HEART challenges are not even considered until the humans are fifteen or sixteen years old.

"Should I tone it down?" Mark asked himself. Oh, this was a hard one. "What if I kill him during the challenge? I know it's no big deal, but this one is different. Why else would they have sent thirty onlookers to handle this Sean? No, I can't kill him. Not now anyways. Oh, what am I thinking? It's just a HEART test."

"Although, if I do things differently, the Council may have me erased, and I'm not going to let that happen." Mark looked at the clock. "Six o'clock. Wow, I've really got to get organized. The kids will start to arrive at Time Management around eight o'clock on Friday." Mark pulled out his little black book. "Let me see, this task calls for a crazy Italian. Joe Silverstone, 555-1333."

Joe answered the phone. "Hello?"

"It's testing time," Mark answered ominously, "and this one is going to have to be a little different. It's for a twelve-year-old boy. It still has to be in the guidelines of a HEART test."

"You're testing a twelve-year-old boy?" Joe replied.

"Well," Mark responded, "the case I'm working is Sean O'Neill and—"

Joe abruptly interrupted him, "Is he the one that everyone is talking about? You know, 'the one'? The one that Oden believes can change the humans' scheduled path?" Joe was really excited. This was the highest profile case he'd ever known or heard about and was all in.

Mark responded, "We need to treat this case no different than any other case. We still do not know for sure if he is the one or a Jumper or if his destiny is to stay a common man. Sean is still young and has not made a move yet. That's why we have to treat this case as if he were just a regular Jumper." Mark continued by instructing Joe that the test needed to be at the Time Management Park with the standard signal 13, no more than thirteen dead or injured.

"What about adult-child ratio and relative-to-nonrelative ratio?" Joe asked. Mark thought for a moment. "Staying within the guidelines of the signal 13, you can take out two relatives. If both sisters show up at the pool, you can focus the test around Luna if needed. She is Sean's favorite, and that will yield the best results from our test."

Joe considered what Mark had said and reviewed the Time Management calendar. He responded, "The test shall then be in the afternoon about one thirty. I will be ready."

"I knew I could count on my crazy Italian to come up with a test on such short notice." Mark grinned. "Sean was not supposed to be tested as a Jumper until he was about sixteen years old, but I am not going to look like a fool in front of James, and there is apparently so much interest in him by other Milkies that it warrants an early test." Mark continued to give himself affirmation, trying to convince himself that he was doing the right thing.

"I understand," Joe replied, "and you will not be disappointed, the test will be as you directed. I assure you."

CHAPTER

4

"Wake up!" Mary called from the kitchen, her voice echoed down the hall of their house. Susan was already awake and sitting at the kitchen table in her blue and white striped swimsuit, eating breakfast. Luna heard her mom's voice echoing down the hall like a herd of buffalo running in a canyon and asked, "Is breakfast ready yet?"

Mary yelled back, "Yes, let's go. It will get cold if you don't hurry!" Sean and Luna came to the kitchen at the same time.

"Pancakes!" Sean exclaimed, "I'd know that smell anywhere. Thanks, Mom."

"Now, Sean, don't eat so much that you can't swim this morning. Remember, there's a big meet this afternoon," Mary told her son tenderly.

Luna chimed in, "Sean's the best swimmer on the team, but that stupid Mr. Goldman won't give Sean a chance to be team captain. Everybody knows that he should be the captain. Why won't you talk to him, Mom?"

Mary responded, "You know it's not my place to tell Mr. Goldman how to run the swim team. Sean will get his chance when he's a little older, maybe a few more years. Everybody eat. We need to get down to the park."

The phone rang, and Mary answered it. It was Jeffery. "Hello? Hey, baby, I'm stuck at work and won't get off until about two…"

Susan could see the face of her mom and knew what her dad was saying. Susan angrily interjected, "Dad, you are going to miss me swim, my relay is at ten this morning!" Even though Mary was on the phone, Jeffery could hear Susan's disappointment in the background.

"Try to make it home as early as you can," Mary said as nicely as she could to Jeffery. Mary put on a fake smile as she faced the kids.

Sean also realized what his Dad was telling his Mom. "Dad, I've got two relays this afternoon. Can you make those?"

Jeffrey hesitated, and then answered, "I have to let you guys go. If there is any chance for me to get off early…tell the kids I'll do my best." Jeffrey spoke hurriedly. "If the kids' meet starts and I am not there yet, tell them I'm coming as fast as I can and to win for Daddy. They'll understand."

Mary shook her head and said quietly, "You say this every month. You know about the swim meets way ahead of time." Mary changed her tone and covered one hand over her mouth. "How about this time making it for at least one of the kids?" Mary quickly turned around, facing the kids with a very sarcastic smile; then with a quick goodbye, Mary hung up.

Mary paused for a moment, remembering that Jeffrey's brother John was Susan's godfather. Without saying anything, Mary knew that Susan was John's favorite niece. Everybody knew that. Mary picked up the phone and called John; John answered the phone immediately.

"Hello? Mary?"

"Hi, John. I was hoping that you could come to the kids' swim meet. Susan is swimming at ten, and Sean is swimming two relays a little later."

"Tell Susan I'll be there," John replied.

Mary said, "Of course, I will tell Sean also that you'll be there."

"Sean doesn't need anyone to boost his ego." John chuckled.

Mary, ignoring the joke, responded worriedly, "Please don't be like your brother. Be there on time, okay?"

"Yes, ma'am," John responded, "I'll see you soon. Bye."

When Mary and the kids arrived at Time Management at eight thirty in the morning, they were being observed by a new Milky— one with no feelings. You might say they're like a robot that has been programmed for a very specific job. Mary had no idea that her family had been followed for nearly four years. No one in or around the O'Neill family knew that a glitch in time at the sorting table would change everything they knew to be. The O'Neill family is like thousands of other families around the world except one thing—it was Sean O'Neill's turn to be tested.

Remember that one or both souls at the sorting table normally die if they touch each other. The Council of Milkies had guarded the sorting of souls for thousands of years, and the connection and unaccompanied journey to earth of these two living souls forced the Council to descend thirty Milkies to follow, assist, interrupt, disrupt, or terminate the human souls named Sean and Paul. Today is test day, and this is part of the system that each and every Jumper will face around their sixteenth birthday.

The O'Neill family had always lived each day like the one that proceeded, completely clueless of the microscope they lived under or what was to come.

Susan climbed out of the car first and started off toward the pool near the gym. Luna and Sean were standing by the car, waiting on their mom. "Come on, Mom," Sean called to her impatiently.

Mary was deep in hopes that Jeffery would show up. "I'm right behind you, go ahead, kids."

They all made their way toward the pool past the bleachers, with Luna staying behind with her mom. Mary could hear the other kids in the stands calling, "Hi, Sean, Hi, Susan," over and over. Mary felt a sick sense in her stomach that something was wrong, but she didn't know what. You know that ache that you can't shake when you think something is going to happen? That itch on your nose? Some people call it a mother's or father's intuition. It is actually a sense that has been developed into humans over hundreds of generations.

Mary and Luna eventually found their seats at the bottom of the bleachers for the best viewing, but Mary couldn't shake that sick sense in her stomach. Susan's meet did not start until ten o'clock, but many of the girls were in the pool doing warm-up laps.

Mark walked by and greeted Mary. "I'm so glad to see that Susan and Sean are here for the swim meet. You know the team really relies on them."

Luna sat up straight and said in a very sharp tone, "Sean is your strongest swimmer and should be captain. Some people just can't see how great he really is."

Mary responded, "Luna, that's enough. Mr. Goldman has reasons for the ones that he chooses as team captains."

Mr. Goldman responded carefully. "I understand the pride you must feel for your brother, Luna, but, actually, the team chooses the captain. I merely influence their decisions. Besides, you never know what the future has for your brother. Hang in there. I see great things ahead for Sean."

After Mr. Goldman walked away, Mary's embarrassment led her to scold Luna. "I told you when Sean's time is up to be captain, he'll be there. Until then, I would like it if you were a little more polite to Mr. Goldman."

Many of the girls were getting out of the water now, including Susan, and getting pep talks from their moms and dads. Susan said, "I'm so excited just before every race. Do you really think that Uncle John will make it here in time?"

Luna answered, "He's not Dad, and Uncle John will be here."

Just then, a voice from the outside the stands called out, "Hey, girls!"

Luna responded, "Uncle John! Not only did he make it, but he's made it on time."

Even though Susan was soaking wet from swimming her practice laps, she still ran up and hugged and greeted her Uncle John, "I knew you'd be here!"

Uncle John responded, "I wouldn't miss you swimming for anything. Do I need to speak to that swim coach of yours and find out where you all are going to celebrate after the swim meet?"

Susan responded with a very coy smile and said, "I'd rather just our family go to lunch after."

Mary chimed in, "I can't afford to pay for everyone. Last swim meet, Jeffrey had to work an extra fifteen hours of overtime just to pay for that lunch."

John said, "Come on, Susan, let's go for a walk. I want to hear that pep talk from your coach. Any idea where Mr. Goldman might be?"

Susan answered, "He's over on the other side of the pool, the one with the big 13 on the front and back of the shirt."

The people at the pool had no way of knowing the real reason that Mark was wearing a shirt with a 13 on the front and back. It was a clear message to all Milkies and any certified Jumpers that he was involved in a HEART testing, and, in case there was other Milkies from other cases at the pool, to let them know that signal 13 was in effect.

Just then, an announcement came over the loudspeaker, "All Bluebird girls four hundred relay race, get to your starting positions!"

Uncle John looked at Susan and said, "I guess we can't get that walk in."

Mary said, "Good luck, Susan! Win it for Daddy!"

Susan was swimming the second leg of the race, standing behind the podium and waiting for the gun to go off.

The starting official raised his gun and then...bang, the race began!

The first girls were in the water, and Susan stepped up on the podium. She looked at the opening between the bleachers in the parking lot, hoping that her dad would make this meet.

Mary yelled out, "Focus, Susan, focus on the water!"

Susan turned, shook off her nervous tension, and started talking to herself, "Pace yourself! It's only one hundred meters." She saw the first swimmer coming, still talking to herself, "Get ready!" and her teammate touched the side of the pool... splash! Into the water she went. Down the pool, Susan swam, and getting to the end, flip, turned, and headed back, swimming faster and faster, with hopes of getting a big enough lead to ensure a team win, reaching out, and touching the wall. The third swimmer jumped in, and Susan climbed out of the water, all smiles. She looked over to the bleachers and...no Daddy. Everybody else was jumping and cheering, but she wanted her Daddy to see how well she did. Susan turned and cheered her teammates on. Faster, faster, everybody was cheering, her team and another were neck and neck for second and third. They were all yelling loudly, faster, faster. At the end, Susan's team finished a close second. They were so excited.

After the initial celebration with her team, Susan ran over to her family. "Uncle John, Uncle John! Did you see how well we did?"

Uncle John and Sean ran over and hugged Susan, "That's the best you've ever done!" Sean exclaimed.

Uncle John said, "Come on! My treat! Let's go to the concession stand and get some lunch.

Mary said, "We have some time. Sean's meet doesn't start until around one thirty."

The line at the concession stand was moving steadily, and everybody was standing around waiting their turns patiently. Uncle John was first in line for the O'Neills turn at the concession stand and pointing to Susan; he smiled and said to the lady in the concession stand, "Give this young lady anything she wants, this is the best swim meet she's had yet."

Susan was smiling from ear to ear. To her, this was the best day she'd ever had. Beautiful sunshine, warm day, and her team came in second. To Susan, the only thing that would make this day better is if her dad had actually made it. Susan whispered to her Uncle John, "It would really be icing on the cake if my team does better than Sean's team." Nobody else heard what Susan whispered, but Susan's laughter was contagious, and it didn't take long before everyone else started laughing.

Susan said, "I'll have a hot dog, some chips, and a large Pepsi."

Uncle John was beaming as though his own daughter had just come in second. He smiled at the concession stand attendant and playfully flirted with her. They gathered their food and some napkins and headed over to the bleachers.

Out in the parking lot, Joe was sitting patiently under an elm tree, smiling and waving at all the parents and kids arriving at the pool. Joe had been at the parking lot since early this morning, using his powers of mental telepathy to get everybody to park in such a way that nothing would impede him from having a very successful signal 13. This was going to be a sporting match. Joe knew that there would be little or no bad attitudes, so his powers of persuasion and mental telepathy would work well. Joe was thinking to himself that this was going to be the best test that he had ever participated in. Emotions were things that a Milky had absolutely no need of. Emotions only show up in Milkies if they have been exposed to humans too long.

Joe definitely did not fit that category. He had been on earth for over fifty years and assisted three potential Jumpers, and none of them passed their HEART test. If he had any kind of emotions at all, he probably would've picked a different way to test Sean, but that's not the case.

Joe was completely focused with no human emotions to get in his way of completing this task. Three successful HEART tests were in his resume, and perfect weather will make this number four. With Joe's planning and with his abilities, he would maximize what was expected of him.

Joe looked at his watch and carefully started going over each and every possible outcome that could happen for Sean's test. His hands were agitating around the steering wheel of his '56 Chevy truck, and he was looking at the crowd, looking at the placement of where he telepathically told Sean's family to sit on the bleachers when they arrived at the pool. Sean was now where he would be around one thirty. Joe looked into the pool area and saw Mark with a big 13 on his back.

He looked at his watch. One o'clock.

Joe started talking to himself, using his mental telepathy. That was Joe's talent. Joe was extremely talented when it comes to mental telepathy; he could make almost anybody do whatever he suggested.

Okay, girls, get away from the edge of the stands! Hey, you! Yes, you, on the third row, go get something to eat. Joe's mental commands had everybody nearly in place. *Five, six, seven, eight, okay!* He started to mentally talk to some of the other people, or should I say, pawns. *What are you doing? You, go to the restroom. Almost everybody is in place, just two more pawns, and it's a go!* Joe started up his truck, making sure that nobody would mess with his focus. He was ready, counted the pawns again, and slowly moved his truck into position. He looked at his watch. One twenty-five, almost ready. Joe heard the loudspeaker. "Junior boys four hundred meter race, go to the starting positions."

Sean was going to start the relay for his team; Sean went over to the third starting block, smiling at his mom.

Joe looked again at his watch. One twenty-nine. He looked up and said, "Time!"

Joe looked around, took another mental note of how many people would be involved. *Check, is Sean in place? Check.*

Joe punched the gas pedal and accelerating toward the corner of the bleachers. He jumped over the curb and across the grass and over the bushes. Nobody saw the truck coming! The truck slammed into the corner of the bleachers where Mary and her family were. Sections of bleachers were flying, people were screaming. It was a perfect strike. Joe knew that if he were playing baseball, this would be a home run. He glanced over at Mark, and Mark gave him the nod of approval. The blood, the screaming, the chaos had no effect on Joe or Mark; they were just doing their job, performing a test. Joe asked Mark telepathically, *Did I hit the mark?*

Mark telepathically responded, *Yes.*

Joe only asked one more question, *Am I finished here?*

Mark responded, *You can go.* And with that, Joe's heart stopped, and he was dead. To the humans, this would look like an old man had a medical emergency like a heart attack.

Sean looked over, and his whole family was gone, and a truck was where his family was sitting. Sean looked around as if time were going in slow motion. People everywhere were screaming and terrified. There were people on the ground with parts of the bleachers sticking in them. Sean's every move and emotion was being monitored, scored, and recorded for the report.

Mark said to himself, *It is hard to believe that this boy is only twelve years old.* Sean seemed to know instinctively what to do among all the confusion and screaming. Sean made his way to the truck and, seeing a body under the vehicle, he started calling for people. "Under here!" Sean called loudly. "Over here, there's somebody under the truck. Help, over here!"

Sean's words went unnoticed because he's just a kid. The screaming and chaos from everywhere drowned out Sean's words.

Sean stared at a bloody lady bellowing in agony. He had no idea who she was, but she was in complete agony. She was pinned partially under the truck and holding on to what she knew was her daughter. She was screaming unrecognizable words, but you knew she was calling for her daughter. Other people were racing to where the truck was. The screaming and chaos was unimaginable. The lady under the truck was just looking at Sean. Then she stopped screaming, her eyes became cold, and her hand let go of the lifeless hand of her daughter. Sean yelled again, but no one answered. While the people started gathering around the truck, Sean was yelling, "Hurry, get her out before she dies."

The lady was gone, and the hand that she was trying to hold wasn't her daughter's, it was a man's. His right arm was nearly torn off, and the right side of his face was completely unrecognizable. He had a terrible stench because his flesh was seared from the heat of the muffler. Sean's world seemed to somehow be running in slow motion as he stared at the lifeless body. Another lady yelled that there was a child under the truck also.

Two people reached under the truck and pulled the lifeless body out. The smell of her burnt flesh and her body covered with blood and grime were terrible; one lady was screaming, "Is she alive?" Her body and head had been crushed and mangled, but the clothes she was wearing was unmistakable. It was Luna! Sean dropped to his knees, and his lips started to quiver. His eyes were welling up, but he couldn't speak. He just looked like a lost soul.

All the screaming and yelling was just rolling off his back. His sister and protector, Luna, was dead! But the words didn't come out; he was speaking but nothing was coming out. One of the parents tried to push him to the side as he stood there lifelessly staring at Luna's clothes when he heard his mother yelling, "Sean, Sean!"

Mary was under a section of the bleachers but alive. Sean was looking for that voice. Where? So many people in so much debris! Sean's face was getting redder by the second with emotions. "Mom! Mom! Where are you?"

Mary was in tremendous pain, with a piece of metal impaling her side. She was losing consciousness, as her blood was coming out of her side where the piece of metal was sticking into her. Sean spotted his mother and headed toward her, trying to get through the pieces of bleachers that were everywhere. Sean got as close as he could.

The mother in Mary tried to come out and comfort Sean but couldn't. She was in too much pain and trapped under a pile of steel.

"Mom! Luna was under the truck, and the people were saying that she was dead…Luna's dead!" The tears that were rolling down her face from the pain now switched to tears of agony. The pain of the piece of steel impaling her was merely a blip in time to her after hearing that her baby was dead. Mary couldn't hold back the pain, and now her heart was in more pain. Her baby girl was gone, and she thought she would be gone also. The pain…she couldn't move. There was so much debris on her, plus that one piece was sticking right through her abdomen.

Mary worked up the strength to ask for Susan. "Sean, find Susan, and your Uncle John." Sean was just looking around and still didn't realize that the first body that they pulled from under the car was Uncle John.

"I don't know," Sean said. Mary was starting to lose consciousness again. She could feel her body losing its temperature. She was getting very lightheaded, and her speech was fading fast. Sean looked around and saw four people in the pool under a section of the bleachers. The swimsuits did not look like the swimsuit Susan was wearing. The water had a pink fog to it. Sean started to jump in but was pushed out of the way by another man. The man was pulling on an arm that was in the water, but the rest of the body was pinned under a section of metal. Sean realized that there were other people in the water also. Time had started to speed up for Sean with the screams of chaos.

Mary was in pain but alive. She knew she was pinned, but then the mother in her said, "It's not my time, you can't have me yet!" Sean turned around, and then his world turned to slow motion again. "Find Susan!" While his world was still in slow motion, he started to be like everyone else and then stopped. His little voice inside his head said, "Find Susan."

A man grabbed Sean and said, "What you are doing? Get with the rest of the kids and stay out of the way."

Sean's world seemed to be programmed like everyone else, the screaming and yelling, the "Somebody, help me over here!" was very loud. Sean's twelve-year-old body couldn't lift the pieces of bleachers and steel, and he felt helpless. Now the sounds of the injured were starting to get drowned out by all the sirens from the oncoming fire rescue.

Sean called out to his Mom, "The firemen are coming, I can see them coming." Mary's body had gone limp under the weight of the bleachers.

Firefighters divided into different teams. To Sean, they seemed like they were well-oiled machines. Some of them were helping the injured, and others were digging the other injured people out. Sean was just standing there, staring at his mother when two firefighters came over and started to dig her out. Sean stared at one firefighter, who was a massive man. The name on his coat said, "Lt. Gabe Dickens." Lieutenant Dickens was looking around for the best way to grab the bleachers when he saw the big 13 on Mark's shirt.

Gabe put his head down and shook it; this was not his first rodeo!

Like thousands of Jumpers before him, Gabe was a Jumper also. His HEART test was twenty-five years ago, and there had been a big 21 on an older lady's shirt. His HEART test had been a very bloody tornado, and because of his size, the Milky had decided Gabe's appropriate gift for him was super strength. Three days after his test, it was explained to him that he would not be just a common man as an adult and that his gift to assure his success in life would be tremendous strength. That he would always have bulldozer strength as long as he used it for the good of humankind.

Gabe knew this was somebody's HEART test but did not know who because he was not a Milky and could not identify who was being tested. He just knew that he would have to do his part.

One firefighter climbed into the twisted bleachers and cut Mary free, and then called for Lieutenant Dickens. The firefighter looked into Mary's eyes and knew time was not on her side. Lieutenant Dickens grabbed the section of the bleachers and, with the strength of ten grown men, lifted the section while the other firefighter slid Mary out. Sean could only just stand there and cry as he watched them work on his lifeless mom.

"We have a pulse!" one of the firemen said, but Mary's whole face was white from the loss of blood. Another firefighter was taping the part of the bleachers that was sticking through her so that it would not move. They couldn't remove it because it could kill her. It was going to the hospital with her. Since the firefighters were trying to get her organized and on a stretcher and into the ambulance, Sean had to let go of her hand. Mary came to for just a second, staring at Sean. She pulled the oxygen mask off to ask about Susan and Uncle John, begging to know what he had seen. Mary knew they had been right next to her and had not seen either one of them since the crash.

A man with a gentle voice was talking to Mary, trying to calm her down. "Ma'am, we will find them, let my men do their job." He seemed to be the boss because everybody came to him for answers, the ambulance people, policeman, and all the other firemen. He never lost his cool, and it was as if his world were able to work in slow motion as Sean's did. His nametag said Captain Ed Whinnery. He was calm and cool, as if he had done this a hundred times. His eyes were kind, and his face was chiseled like a marine.

The reason Captain Whinnery was so calm was because he had done this over and over in his life. He was a World War II marine veteran, and during a bloodied ambush, he was wounded and used his own body to shield his wounded lieutenant from a machine gun nest. Ed was shot eleven times and survived; the two of them were the only survivors on both sides of the ambush. Ed saved his lieutenant, and then his Lieutenant dragged him to safety.

The firefighters were bringing people out one after another, people screaming on stretchers, yet no Susan and Uncle John. Sean started to walk over to the area where the truck was sitting. There was a white sheet lying over something. Captain Whinnery turned Sean around and told him to stay with his mom. Sean knew that it only had been minutes since the crash, but it seemed like hours. He was mentally drained, and then he noticed the swimsuit on the stretcher going by…it was Susan!

Mary could also see the blood all over the bandages, and two legs wrapped up like a mermaid. Mary struggled to see who was on the stretcher, but there was no way she could see. She had a mask on her face and a piece of steel taped to her abdomen and IV tubes sticking out of her arm. She just lay there as if she were sleeping while they loaded her into the ambulance. The mama in Mary knew that the person on the stretcher was Susan. Mary felt herself passing out, and now thoughts of Susan put her trauma over the top. Mary passed out.

Two ambulances left, and then three more arrived. By this time, Mark had all the kids together waiting for parents or loved ones to come get them. The time was going by so slowly, and the crying and screaming were slowly settling down. Sean saw a very familiar and scared face coming toward him. It was his Dad, coming for him.

Jeffrey grabbed Sean and hugged him, then started talking to Mr. Goldman. "I heard about the accident on the radio and came straight over. Where's my family?"

Mr. Goldman had a dumb look on his face. Jeffrey repeated himself, a little louder this time. "Where is my family!"

Mr. Goldman responded, "You will have to talk to Captain Whinnery. Everything happened so fast, and I'm not sure where they were taken."

Captain Whinnery was not going anywhere but was stepping into his truck with a clipboard when he saw Sean and Jeffrey coming up to his truck. Jeffrey said, "Captain, please tell me where has my family been taken and what happened."

Captain Whinnery responded, "Slow down! Who are you looking for?"

Jeffrey said, "My wife and my kids! How did this happen?"

"As of right now, it appears that a man may have had a heart attack and lost control of his truck, crashing into the bleachers at the pool," Captain Whinnery said.

Jeffrey said, "My wife, Mary O'Neill, and my two daughters, Susan and Luna, are missing. Please! Tell me you know something."

The captain said, "Did you say your last name was O'Neill?"

Sean was holding onto his Dad with his arms wrapped around him. He wanted to scream Luna's dead, but no words would come out. Captain Whinnery got out of his truck with the clipboard and looked up at Jeffrey. "I'm sorry to tell you..."

Before Captain Whinnery could even finish his sentence, Jeffrey dropped to the ground and started crying. Captain Whinnery composed himself and continued, "Mary was taken to the hospital. I am sorry to tell you that your daughter Luna didn't make it. She was crushed under the truck, as well a man named John O'Neill. Was he a relation to you as well?"

Jeffrey looked up, crying, and said, "John? John was here, and John's dead too? That's my baby brother!" Jeffrey nearly passed out with grief.

Captain Whinnery was aware that John could have been Jeffrey's brother, but he was thinking of how to get through the rest of this bad news. How much more bad news could this man take. "Your wife and daughter Susan were taken to St. John's Hospital. I can arrange for a ride for you and your son if you need me to."

Jeffery's ears seemed to be filled with water and cotton balls; nothing else was getting through, only muffled words that did not mean anything to him.

The rest of the whole world just disappeared from Sean's eyes. All he could see through his tears was his dad on his knees, uncontrollably crying. Sean looked up and saw Captain Whinnery wiping a tear from his face.

Captain Whinnery didn't know how big or how small their family was, but this man had just lost a brother and a daughter, and his wife and other daughter were in the hospital, and the young man in front of them had just witnessed it all.

Captain Whinnery, with the heart and soul of seemingly many men, looked helplessly at Jeffrey. With this much bad news to give to one person, composure just doesn't happen. Jeffrey looked up and asked, "Tell me about my wife and Susan, how bad are they?"

Captain Whinnery responded that they were on their way to the hospital. "Your wife was under a section of the bleachers. She has multiple wounds from the bleachers and has lost some blood." Captain Whinnery hesitated for a moment.

"Well, what about Susan?" Jeffrey called out.

"Susan was unresponsive, and her legs were pinned between some larger debris at the concession stand. You need to go to the hospital and be with them."

CHAPTER 5

Mark was left standing alone at Time Management looking around at the damage and going over in his mind how the day unfolded knowing he could do nothing more.

He decided to drive back to his house, and he brought Martha, the school principal and on the same Jumper case with him, for the debriefing that would follow a signal 13. He went over all the details perfectly. *Okay, signal 13 was invoked, and injuries and deaths stayed within the parameters. I know I'm ready for the Council.* The sky was getting dark, really dark. A storm was approaching, but it was not a normal storm. This storm was a concentrated cloud bank. Mark was approaching his house when the heavy lightning started striking the ground, and six bolts of lightning hit the ground on the lawn. The light show revealed six of the members of the Council of Milkies. Mark was quite surprised that six of the council members came down for the debriefing.

The Council is made up of hundreds of council members who are all equal except for the Supreme Councilman and the councilman in charge of the weather. The Supreme one is named Malaywah, and he wields the most powerful staff in existence. The second-in-charge is Zimbabwe, and he wields a powerful staff as well. The Council members were easily distinguishable from an ordinary Milky because they all had such an icy appearance; you could say their skin was nearly translucent. Upon receiving their commission, the new council members were tapped on the side of their head by Malaywah's staff to give them the utmost clarity to make decisions as well as an unbiased ability to pass judgment. However, having the staff touch the side of their head transforms the iris in one eye to a clear crystal appearance. All Milkies recognize a council member's eyes immediately.

As Mark stepped out of his car, one of the council members named Oden came up to him. Oden said in a calm manner, "We all need to go inside of your dwelling." Just then, a loud and very bright bolt of lightning hit the ground. It was Malaywah in person, the Supreme Council Leader and number one in charge of the Council. Malaywah had a large scar on the side of his face from the battle in 1820, in which he overthrew Nyomee the Third. She had nearly beheaded him when she grazed him across the face with the royal staff. The six council members and Mark all dropped to one knee. Malaywah spoke, "This is a debriefing I want to hear in person for myself."

As they all were heading for the door, Mark started to have second thoughts about how the test had gone. Upon entering the home of Mark, Malaywah paused for a moment then tapped his staff on the floor, making Mark's floor turn to a crystal-like appearance. This completed the connection from the Council chamber to earth. Then Malaywah said, "Now I feel more at home."

Mark was looking at the floor, which had the appearance of leaded glass, but it felt like he was walking on a normal floor. Mark had never seen anything like this on earth. He felt like he was walking in the clouds. This was only the first debriefing that Mark had attended. Mark looked up and said, "It's a pleasure to have all of you here, but I was only expecting one council member."

Malaywah sat quietly at the head of the table with his staff in his hand. Malaywah didn't say a word—just sat there. The seats to the right and left of him were empty. Not even the other council members wanted to be too close to his staff. Respect was an understatement; Malaywah was in a category all his own when one thinks about power. A broad observation would be that Milkies did not show emotions; however, just being in the presence of Malaywah's staff makes anyone, or should I say everyone, nervous. Malaywah may look like an average Milky councilman, but that staff visually sets him apart from any other councilman. The staff is like an electrically charged crystal light rod with a crystal cloud on the top of it.

Oden, as the third in charge, responded to Mark's greetings, "We are here today because you invoked a signal 13 in the name of a twelve-year-old human named Sean O'Neill."

Mark responded, "I have been closely observing Sean for over a year, and I believe that he may be a threat larger than just a Jumper. A Jumper!" he stuttered again.

"This human," Oden interrupted, "the boy was only twelve years old. Why would you be invoking a signal 13?"

Mark responded, "When I first met Sean, he was nearly five years old and was already showing signs of strength and leadership far above his age. When he was at the pool, he was always doing one of two things. First, he is physically stronger than any other boy his age. Second, he is helping the other kids with their swimming techniques, even the older boys and girls. Just something is different about him," Mark blurted out. "A human with these qualities at that age is not going to settle for the class he was given. I was the one that flung him onto the side of the Mount Soul. I had never seen a human soul cling on to another human soul and live. I have observed Sean, and I believe that both Sean and Paul, because of how long they made contact into the Mount Soul, that drive to live will turn into something very dangerous."

Oden responded, "Contact was made, actual contact? Both lived?"

"Yes," Mark responded, "from my vantage point, I saw that the soul named Sean was trying to use the human soul named Paul as a climbing tool. I believe that he may be able to absorb other Jumpers' abilities. I believe he may be like a human energy leech."

Felicia was the smallest on the Council but spoke the most directly. "Give us the results of the signal 13." Felicia was all business, no small talk.

Mark responded, "Sean's uncle, John O'Neill, Sean's sister, Luna, and Joe Silverstone, who conducted the signal 13, and five others all died. Five others were taken to the hospital. Sean's mother and other sister Susan were two of the five that were taken to the hospital.

Malaywah, with a stern look on his face, said, "Why was the contact at the Mount Soul never reported? Your initial report stated that there was a situation, not contact. You never mentioned contact in the report. The last time we had contact like this, and they both lived was around the year 406. One of those human souls was Attila. Attila had hit the side of Mount Soul and was trying to pull himself up. He pulled off another soul, and then tried to fight off two of our own Milky Guards before being removed from the top. The contact alarm was sent out, and I banished him to the darkest part of earth. Attila the Hun, as he became known, was a thorn in my side for forty-seven years before I had him eliminated on his wedding night in the year 453."

Malaywah stood up. "Members of the Council, we are not going to go through this again." Taking his staff and pointing it, he said, "Mark, if you hold back any more information from the council, you won't be returning to the heavens. Instead, I'll turn you to dust."

Oden was looking at Mark and said, "At the present time, do you think the signal 13 was fair to be used on Sean? Mark?"

Mark nervously responded, "I hope it was enough to determine his worth as a Jumper. I believe he is a very strong soul. During the test, Sean didn't lose control. All the other kids and the adults were screaming and crying in panic. If you wish me to assist you with the debriefing in three days, what gift are you going to bestow upon him?"

Oden was telepathically communicating with the other council members, and then he spoke out loud. "None at this time. He needs to be watched for a time and retried at sixteen like all other Jumpers. The fact that he made contact and lived tells us that a gift needs to be considered thoughtfully, but nothing for now."

Felicia responded, "I think we need to protect him. He is vulnerable now that Luna is gone. From what you have reported the last couple of years, in Sean's eyes, Luna was his guardian. I think you may have taken out the wrong sister, and I hope this one doesn't come back and bite us. If my memory serves me correctly, Attila acted the same way. A sense of calm surrounded him even after he was granted any enhancement. It sounds like his soul has the same drive or at least an eerie resemblance to that of Attila."

Pointing at Mark, Malaywah responded, "What about the other soul, Paul, has he been located yet?" Malaywah knew that someone in the Council must be coveting Paul; how else could Paul stay undetected for so many years. Malaywah stared around. The entire room stayed quiet.

Malaywah said sternly and stood up, "Find him, and when you do, keep him away from Sean." Malaywah paused for a moment then pointed his staff at Mark. "You and Martha need to keep us informed. I don't like surprises. This meeting is adjourned."

The entire Council stood up. Malaywah put his hand on top of the staff, and the entire Council faded like a cloud into the crystal floor. Malaywah and the Council were gone, but his point was crystal clear to Mark and Martha.

Martha said, "No enhancement for Sean? But he not only survived his test, he stayed strong. He should have been given something, I know he's only twelve, but he did survive his test."

Mark responded, "I'm not going against what Malaywah said in any shape or form. You heard Oden, and besides, I think I'm right. I do believe that he may be able to absorb other abilities from other people. He gives off that feeling like a piece of steel going by a magnet. We need to make sure that he does not stay too close to us for any amount of time. Sean is starting to go through puberty, and this is the time in their development when the abilities of humans start to show up in our Jumpers."

Martha responded, "Do you really think he can absorb our ability? What about our ability to incinerate? At twelve years old, his body could not support that kind of power."

Mark responded, "Do you really want to know, or should I say, do you really want to find out? Do you really think that Sean would get supercharged if he were to make contact again with Paul? Malaywah was very direct, if there is any sign of Paul in the area, we need to keep them apart."

Martha said, "I would kind of like to see a supercharged human like Attila. I mean, think about it…Attila passed his HEART test, and his enhancement made him a legend."

Mark interrupted, "Life didn't work out so good for Attila. Remember he tried to make himself a czar. Attila did not make it inside of Mount Soul like Caesar. We have to treat Sean as a Jumper. I'll bring you back home, and we will meet up at the pool tomorrow and start moving forward."

James was reflecting on the events of the day. He had driven by the Time Management pool and seen Mark walking around earlier in the day with a big 13 on his shirt. Neither Martha nor Mark had contacted him to be part of the invoking of signal 13. The real reason why nobody contacted him was because James was devolving into a regular human, and all the other Milkies could sense it. The signal that he gives off as a Milky was getting very weak. He couldn't feel the presence of other Milkies either. During the test, all he could do was watch the events of the testing take place. He kept his eyes on Mark throughout the test, hoping for a chance to make him a casualty, but no such luck. Mark observed from a safe distance and documented everything for the council. As the ambulance left with Mary, James followed it to the hospital and into the emergency room.

James went back outside, and now that he knew where Sean's mother and sister were, he had to plot out a new way to think of how he could gain charge of Sean. He didn't know why he was feeling so bitter at the O'Neill family, but with every moment passing, he was becoming completely obsessed with them.

Several days passed, and James was at the hospital again. *This will be the next place that I can make my move*, James thought. With every minute passing, James was losing his ability to operate as a Milky.

James stood in the hallway outside of Susan's room. Jealousy and rage were racing through his mind. Negative emotions like these eat away at a Milky's powers, making them more and more human every minute. James was muttering to himself, "How dare Mark take the lead when it should have been me in charge. Signal 13 states that only thirteen are allowed to either be injured or die, but nobody would notice if the mama died. Who's to say?" James had been wearing his Georgetown sheriff's uniform. It had only taken a year to force himself into this position using his powers of persuasion on the mayor to assign him into the position as sheriff. Now that position was going to pay huge dividends! James knew that a position like sheriff would give him easy access to human trust. James went back into the hospital, and without any trouble, stepped in to Susan's room. He saw her lying on the bed. She was still asleep with an oxygen mask on and an IV in her forearm. "How is she doing?" he asked the nurse, only because she was in there, not because he actually cared.

"The swelling in her leg had finally gone down enough that we might be able to do surgery on one of her legs, but it doesn't look good. We are waiting on the doctor to review the CT scan for today. We are getting an operating room ready so that we can get the blood circulating in that leg and put the bones back together," the nurse responded. "Did you see the accident scene? We were told that it was really bad." The nurse continued to small talk, but to James, it was just *blah, blah, blah, blah, blah.*

James was trying to focus his mental telepathy on the nurse, but it wasn't working. James had devolved to the point where his mental telepathy had very little ability, and the human primal side was growing. The primal instinct is the emotion that overpowers all other emotions…survival! James was developing has first emotion.

James said, "I saw the aftermath, and it wasn't good at all. In fact, I'm surprised that only a few were killed. What about her?" he asked, pointing to Susan.

"I think she has a good chance but not sure that she will walk again. But it's going to be a long road," said the nurse. "She is so young, I hope she makes a full recovery. I gave her a sedative, and hopefully, we get a green light for surgery."

James could only think of one thing—shut up and get out!—but continued to give the fake smile at the nurse.

The nurse said, "I need to go see if the chart has been updated. With any luck, we will be heading for the operating room in a few minutes. I'll be right back." The nurse smiled at the sheriff and headed out the door.

James's mind was racing now, knowing that he was all alone with Susan. He looked around the room for an empty syringe, telling himself to inject the IV line with air. Air will travel completely undetected, and she will be dead within the hour. James started rifling through the cabinets. *Come on! Really! What is the sense of having all these drawers if you don't put anything in them? There has to be something here I can use.* He opened another drawer and another…then a door, still nothing useful. He kept looking in other drawers and finally found a syringe. Yes! James fumbled with the syringe packaging, trying to open it. Finally, he quickly went over to the bedside.

"Sheriff," a voice called out to him. James cloaked the syringe and turned around.

"Yes?" he responded.

It was Jeffrey. He asked, "How is she doing?"

James responded with a completely fake smile, "I'm going to find out how this happened. She is so young." James stepped away from the bed.

Jeffrey and Sean stepped up to the bed. "Oh, my baby, wake up, Susan, Daddy's here!" After nearly a week, Jeffrey was still a complete wreck. Jeffery was a very strong man, but that also came with strong emotions. James quietly walked out of the room, furious with himself that he missed such an easy opportunity.

He spoke quietly under his voice, "You're not out of the woods yet, girl. If I can't get to you, then I know somebody who can." Just then, the back of his right ear was starting to burn, like someone stuck him with a hot poker. James rubbed on it but couldn't stop the burning. He headed into the men's room thinking that cold water would soothe the burning. He looked in the mirror and started to see himself differently. He was changing, without realizing that his actions had fast forwarded his transformation from a Milky to just a human. He pulled his ear back and looked and could see a red rash. The M1113 was gone, leaving behind nothing but red rash. James was now on his own as a human. His greed and self-righteous attitude had transformed him into a normal human. He kept looking at the rash and telling himself, "What the hell is that?" That was one ugly rash. However, the cool water was not making it feel better. A man came out of the stall and started to wash his hands next to James. James looked at the man in the mirror. A cold chill ran down his back. James felt fear like he had never felt it before.

James said, "You...you look familiar, do I know you?" James stared into Oden's eyes, and the fear was overwhelming. James was trembling, frozen in place as he started to urinate in his pants. James tried to turn around, but his feet would not move. James stared into Oden's eyes and was frozen in place as Oden extended one fingernail that resembled a syringe and inserted it into the corner of James's eye, penetrating deep into his brain.

Oden stepped closer, ever so slowly, looked at James, and said, "Not in this lifetime." Oden had completely erased all of James's memory of being a Milky. "Take care of that rash. You don't want to get an infection."

Even though James was wearing his sheriff's uniform, he was terrified of Oden, and as soon as he could move, James hurriedly walked out of the men's room with a puzzled look on his face and urine down his leg and into a shoe. James's heart was racing; then another cold chill came across him.

"What if that man heard me talking about Susan, he could tell somebody," he muttered to himself. Something about that guy scared him or, should I say, terrified him. His eyes, his voice, something about him seemed like he could rip your soul out. James put his hand on his gun and went back into the men's room, but Oden was gone.

Mark called Martha, "You need to come over, we need to talk." Martha said, "On my way."

Martha arrived at Mark's house, and as she got out of the car, she could see in the daylight where the Council had made their entrance. The lawn was burnt up. She thought to herself that the Council sure made an entrance. and it was easy to find where they have been. She opened the door and nervously walked in. The floor was still warm. Then she heard Mark babbling.

Overnight, Mark was dissecting everything that the Council had been talking about. Mark said, "The Council is a little worried that we may have taken out the wrong sister. Susan was like a bossy director and somebody that Sean was not always able to connect closely to. Luna, on the other hand, was like the big sister, protective but loving, and now that protective and loving side is gone."

Martha said, "Do you think the Council wants us to take Susan out also? Is that what you're saying?"

"No, but we need to keep a close watch on Sean. The Council was talking about another man who was very similar to Sean. Do you remember them talking about what happened about two thousand years ago, like it just happened? Remember them talking about Attila? Malaywah sent him from birth to the darkest place on earth, but yet he still rose from a poor nomad to a powerful emperor. Malaywah said that he did not want this to turn into a case like that again."

"Mark, I was there at the meeting with you, what's going on? Are you losing it? I heard what Malaywah said. Are you okay?"

Mark started to speak with a strange look on his face—overanalyzing the meeting was the likely answer.

Just then, a light came through the floor, and Oden appeared. Mark dropped to one knee, and then Martha did the same. Mark said, "Oden, I wasn't expecting you."

Oden said, "Sean has a formidable nemesis, a former Milky that has gone rogue, the Georgetown sheriff, James."

Martha said, "Mark and I know all about him. He was very angry when he found out that he was not going to be the lead of Sean."

Oden said, "He has already tried once to eliminate Susan, and he probably will not stop. He is a very disturbed human, and in his human position as sheriff, he is going to be very dangerous to Sean. The two of you will have to take on this case together from this point out. The Council is watching 850,085 cases just in just North America. Of those cases, 850,083 are simple Jumper cases. These are simple, just guide them along and keep them developing. A Milky's job is clear—overseeing the human that they are assigned and steer them along. The other two cases are connected, Sean and Paul. Paul…a Milky or a group of Milkies are hiding him. You two need to make sure that their paths never cross. Both of you have been warned about James and will keep the Council informed." As he had done before, Oden faded like a cloud into the crystal floor.

It had been two months since signal 13 was set into motion with Sean. As per the orders of Oden, neither Mark nor Martha had spoken to Sean about the test. Martha had tried several times to figure a way to explain what happened to Sean but did not dare to cross Oden.

Mary had been home for over a month recovering from her surgery, and Susan was scheduled to come home today.

Jeffrey was at home and looked at the clock. "Sean, let's go. We don't have all day! We have to get to the hospital by ten to bring Susan home."

Sean hadn't been himself since the accident; he didn't understand why Luna was taken, or why he didn't even have a scratch. Sean came into the kitchen. "Do I have to go to the hospital?"

Mary responded, "You can stay home with me if you want, I have to get the house ready and hang the welcome home sign."

Sean sat down at the table, unaware of the fury that has been brewing over the past two months. To Sean, it was just another day, which will probably start with the same question...why? The truck crashing at pool was something that Sean could not get out of his brain. *If Uncle John and Luna had been with him, they would've been fine? Why weren't they with me?* Sean's little brain just would not be quiet. He felt like it just wasn't fair.

CHAPTER

6

For over ten years in Canada, the council had been having a different kind of problem. They had had fifteen Milkies go missing. Each one of them had responded to possible sightings of Paul.

Georgia Yellowstone, like all other Milkies, reported to the Council. Her report, over ten years ago, had been that they had found the soul that they were looking for, and he had been named Paul Alexander and that he was living near Montréal.

Albert and Roberta Alexander had seven children, and Paul was the youngest. Albert, or Al as he liked to be called, worked at the local paper mill, and Roberta went by the name Birdie. Her entire job was taking care of six healthy children, all girls. Now comes along a boy; Birdie never thought she would have a son. Paul was not just a son; he was a time thief to an entire family in need of constant care. They had been living paycheck to paycheck with no aspirations of anything better, and then Paul came along. Paul screwed up everything as far as making it. Getting by was now just an unobtainable dream. Paul was different than all the other kids. He was born with a large claw-like birthmark on his back that was outlined with white hair; the doctor that delivered him gasped when Paul was born. If that wasn't enough, Paul's hands and feet were heavily webbed together.

Al was only able to afford the surgery to cut the webbing out of Paul's fingers but couldn't afford to also do his toes. The doctor that Al picked would have been considered a quack. (No pun intended.) The surgeon that performed this procedure did a quick and sloppy job on Paul's fingers, leaving the fingers all with horrible scars and small lumps under the skin.

Al's pride was the real reason he chose to only correct Paul's fingers and not his feet. He told Birdie they couldn't afford it, but that wasn't the real reason. Pride, or lack of it, was the better word. He couldn't stand the fact that he produced a boy that wasn't a typical or a genetically produced perfect son.

Birdie was in charge of the budget, and the hospital bills were making the budget spiral out of control. They were going deeper and deeper in debt. Al could only think of one way to break the cycle, which was to get rid of the time and money thief, Paul!

When Paul was just a year old, Al forced Birdie to drop Paul off at the truck stop near Niagara Falls so that nobody would know where he came from. She left a note, simply saying, "His name is Paul, and I can't deal with him any longer."

Georgia was one of the original thirty Milkies that had been sent to find Paul and Sean. When a Milky is first sent through the sorting table, they are full of drive for their mission, like a team player that just received a pep talk from their coach and sent out on the field. Georgia was no different. Like the other twenty-nine, she wanted to find either Paul or Sean and guide them as the Council directed them. Normally, a Milky escorts the soul through the sorting table into their new bodies, and normally, a Milky has years to report back and forth with the Council on the possible Jumper's progress in life. Paul went an entire year without being located, and then once he was finally located, he was identified as abandoned.

This was how Georgia found him! Nearly frozen and starved, she knew that she had to do something.

She picked him up. This would be Georgia's downfall, knowing that her role as an onlooker was to guide this human, not make physical contact; but this baby had something that just grabbed a hold of her soul…if a Milky had a soul.

She studied Paul. He looked like a regular baby; she smelled it, and it smelled like a regular baby. Paul's hair was snow white. In his eyes were deep oceans of blue. She didn't know why, but he gave off a strange vibe. She thought to herself, *How could someone just get rid of their baby? It's just a baby.*

Georgia sent out a message to the Council, explaining that she had found Paul, and he was near death. Oden sent out a message to the other Milkies that had been sent to locate Paul, "Unless you are involved in a case, and you are within five hundred miles of Montréal, Canada, go to assist Georgia Yellowstone. She has located Paul."

From the time Georgia found Paul, fourteen Milkies had finished their assignments and responded to the message from Oden. Zimbabwe also read the message and had plans of his own for Paul. Zimbabwe had been around for hundreds of years on the Council and had never seen a powerful human such as a czar. Knowing the fact that Paul and Sean both survived contact before the entry into the sorting table told him that these two would be different. He was hoping to cultivate a czar for himself, a super powerful human.

Zimbabwe was a member of the Council and in the position of the second-most powerful staff of the Council. Among other things, the staff gave him the power to move and adjust the jet streams. Malaywah was the one who nominated him for this prestigious spot because he had the stomach to induce human carnage if he was asked to, no questions asked and without any hesitation.

Zimbabwe's staff even demanded respect by the other members on the Council. Very few of the other council members were in contact with him because of his special abilities with the weather.

Even though he looked similar to all the other members of the Council, other council members had a fear or respect of him. His face and hands had the battle scars from using such a powerful staff, and over the decades, his left eye was nearly black while the other was crystal-like from his first appointment.

Zimbabwe contacted two Milkies that he called Elites, with very special skills who had been on earth for nearly four hundred years and were constantly being used by the Council and Zimbabwe to do unscrupulous and off-the-book type operations. The first Elite Zimbabwe chose to call was Eileen Huang; she was his first call for many reasons. Whenever there was someone that needed to be hidden, she was the correct one for the job. She had been honing her skills in the Orient for over two hundred years, and nobody could steer a child to be invisible better than she could.

Tran Lan was Zimbabwe's next call. Tran had been working side by side with Zimbabwe and other members of the Council on nearly all the off-book missions for nearly four hundred years. He specialized in mortal combat and the art of assault. Basically, he was a killing machine, and whenever he got a call, bad things happened.

Zimbabwe met up with Eileen and Tran to tell them of his plan for Paul. Eileen was to make Paul disappear, teach Paul all the Oriental disciplines, and make him multilingual. Tran's job was to make anyone who came looking for Paul disappear until Zimbabwe tells him to stop, or it's time for his HEART test. The disappearances would start with Georgia.

Tran and Eileen had their orders and set off to find Georgia. Georgia would be the first of many strange disappearances over the next few years.

Elaine and Tran moved Paul from place to place and country to country over the next years, always trying to stay one step ahead of the Council and stay on Zimbabwe's good side.

Eileen gave each job a handle name depending on how extreme the job was that they were doing for Zimbabwe. This one she called, in English, the Misfit Prince because there was nothing in her native tongue of Mandarin to explain this child. Just one look at Paul, and Eileen knew that this child was going to have many challenges—the botched-up surgery on his fingers that left his fingers with these terrible scars, not to mention the giant claw scar across his back and webbed feet, but the worst scar of all was that he would have to have to deal with the fact that he was dumped on the side of the road and basically left for dead. That's a tough thing for a child to have to deal with, knowing that someone not only did not want you, but also left you for dead all alone in the cold on the side of the road.

Forward in time to the present: James White had been busy. He had been in touch with some of the lowest of lowlifes in the area. James's new best friend was Mike Bass. Mike was that kid who always cheated his way through life, never earning anything that he was given. Mike would force the girls in school into doing all his assignments. At the age of sixteen, Mike had to make what should have been a life changing decision: join the local fire department to keep from going into jail as a plea agreement for setting a wooden bridge on fire.

The local judge had a strange way to make offenders see the wrong in that they did. For example, Mike had been convicted of committing arson. So the judge gave him a choice of four years working with the fire department or four years in jail. Even though Mike had been kicked out of school in eleventh grade, he still had enough smarts to go to work for the fire department as opposed to going to jail. After he served his mandatory four years with the fire department, he liked it so much, he tried out and was hired for real.

Even though Mike never earned a single rank in the fire department, he screwed over all his buddies to where he was the one that always got promoted and ended up being assistant chief and then he retired. Mike was a professional backstabber. Mike could go out to lunch with the mayor, and on the way out the door, sell the mayor's daughter a bag of weed and a half dozen LSD patches. This was James's number one pick as a best friend. Now you understand why he was James's number one pick as buddy.

James had been playing buddy-buddy with Mike in hopes that Mike could do his dirty work: take out Sean and his entire family. James had no idea why he so hated the O'Neill family, but it totally possessed his every waking moment. To him, the O'Neill family was like a virus, and he wanted to be the doctor to cure it. This morning, James had driven by Jeffrey's house and saw the big sign hanging from the front porch, "Welcome home, Susan!"

That sign was like somebody putting on a bee suit, zipping it up, velcroing all the openings close, and then releasing an entire hive of yellow jackets to the inside of the suit. James's blood pressure was on fire.

Oden knew that James was damaged upon entry to earth and figured that wiping his mind would make him be a regular human, but he was wrong. All that was left is the emotion that humans are born with—to survive. That, of course, explained why James found it much more enjoyable hanging out with Mike. As a survivor, it just felt right being mean! Besides, as police, it came naturally to do things and have nobody question him.

James was like a dog with rabies foaming at the mouth now that Susan would be home. James continued to stare at the sign and finally thought about it. He felt that this could be a golden opportunity to take out all the O'Neills at the same time. James pulled off the road and went into the woods with binoculars, just waiting for everyone to leave for the hospital so he could break into the house and come up with a plan that was foolproof.

Jeffrey came out of the house and called back to Mary, "I love you, and we will be home soon."

James was out of sight but yet close enough to hear. James was furiously talking to himself as he was watching Mary go back into the house. "Why aren't they all going to the hospital? God! I hate those O'Neills! It's almost like somebody's watching out for them. I don't care if it takes another year…I will rid the earth of these O'Neills, even if I have to take them one by one." James came out of the woods and back into his car and drove away.

Jeffrey pulled up to the hospital. He was so excited that Susan was finally coming home. Susan had a long recovery, with damage to both legs, and the right leg was amputated at the knee. "Today Susan is going to have a good day," Jeffrey said to himself. "Even the weather is beautiful." Jeffrey strolled into the hospital with a smile so big, you would've thought that he was the sun. You could see it from one end of the hospital to the other. As Jeffrey walked by, he said the same thing to every nurse, "My girl is coming home today!"

The head nurse stopped Jeffrey and told him that she didn't think that his smile was big enough. Jeffrey grinned even bigger, and then from around the corner, he heard Susan come rolling out, "Daddy!" she yelled.

Jeffrey's eyes were welling over as the tears of joy rolled down his face! "We're going home, baby!"

Now the head nurse was crying. The nurses were accustomed to these kinds of happy moments, especially when a patient has been at the hospital for this long. The nurse that was pushing the wheelchair was laughing and crying at the same time. If Susan's smile were a light, she would've blinded everybody as they headed out the door. As they were loading Susan into the car, Jeffrey got one of those feelings—you know, the one where you feel like someone is watching you, or that cold chill down your back for no apparent reason.

Jeffrey started looking around. He always had that "what if" thought that this could not have been an accident. Jeffrey was looking around; he spotted a black car across the road with blacked-out windows. Jeffrey's imagination started to race; his mind was imagining like a TV detective. The people in that car were taking pictures of him and Susan! Jeffrey stared at the car and stood up. Jeffrey imagined that they stopped taking pictures, but something was really creepy about this. Jeffrey started to walk across the street toward the car, but it pulled off. Jeffrey looked for a license plate, but there was not one to be found.

The nurse called out, "Mr. O'Neill, are you okay?"

Jeffrey responded, "That was really weird. I am sure that those two men were taking pictures of me and Susan. Have you ever seen a car like that before, here at the hospital?"

The nurse responded, "I didn't see the car, so I'm not sure what you are talking about. Are you sure you're okay?"

Jeffrey got in his car and put on a big fake smile for Susan. "Let's go home, baby girl." As they were driving, Jeffery could not shake the black car out of his mind.

"Home! I miss home," Susan said as they pulled away from the hospital and headed for home. Susan stared out the window all the way home and into the driveway, saying, "Not the way I planned on spending my senior year from school."

Susan had so many complications at the hospital that she was the last one from the accident to go home. Miss Ruby decided that since school was starting soon, this would be a good chance to check on Sean. When Miss Ruby arrived at the O'Neill house, it was a party-like atmosphere. Ms. Ruby was greeted at the door by Sean.

"Hello, Sean," said Miss Ruby. "I came over to check on you and your sister." Mary came up behind Sean and welcomed her.

"I hope it is okay for me to come over," Miss Ruby said.

Mary responded, "Of course…come in."

Miss Ruby tried to make a joke. "Okay, Susan! Now that you have this fancy new chair, there's no reason for you to be late for class." Everybody laughed, including Susan.

"Is there anything I can do for you or Sean?" Miss Ruby asked.

Jeffrey said, "I think they're both going to be fine."

Sean was being very quiet and just inquisitively looking at Miss Ruby. This made Miss Ruby a little nervous. She smiled at Sean, and he just kept looking from her feet to her head and from one shoulder to the other.

Miss Ruby patted Sean on the shoulder and said, "I'm going to go ahead and get going. I just want to make sure that the kids would be in school this semester."

Jeffrey walked Miss Ruby to the door, "Take care of those kids, and I'll see them in school," Miss Ruby addressed Jeffery. "If you and the missus need anything, feel free to call me."

Miss Ruby walked away with a perplexed look on her face. *Why was Sean studying my face so hard? Could it be a boy crush on his teacher? Could this be the start of some kind of ability because of Sean's contact at the sorting table? What kind of ability would he be developing? Could the accident have supercharged his ability before puberty?* So many thoughts were going through Martha Ruby's head, but the main thought was just one word: Sean.

CHAPTER 7

Eileen had just arrived in Madrid, Spain, and was buying tickets for herself, Tran, and Paul to go back to Canada. She felt like she had been on the wrong side of Paul's development for over four years because of Zimbabwe. They had been trying to treat Paul as a regular common boy, but that had not been easy. Paul had been like a sponge, absorbing knowledge from everyone that he had made direct contact with, and he was vividly aware that he had been developing powers since he was eight years old. Tran had first started teaching Paul discipline, and when Paul drew blood on Tran's leg with his nails, Paul's eyes lit up, and a surge of energy entered him. Somehow, when Paul draws blood from someone else, it increases his strength. There was no doubt that Paul was going to be a Jumper and not just an orphan struggling through life. Eileen knew that this needed to be kept from everyone, and Tran agreed.

Paul drew blood two more times that same year, fighting two more boys, both times growing stronger and stronger. Without saying anything to Eileen, Tran had transferred a piece of his power by allowing Paul to absorb some of his blood, ensuring Paul's success; Tran was putting every minute into training Paul. Tran was always focused on developing Paul in a manner that pleased Zimbabwe. There was no question in Tran's mind—brute force was the gift Zimbabwe had in mind for this boy. Developing the next czar. This was definitely going to be his superpower—a sure path on which Paul will jump his way through life.

Over the past few years, Eileen found herself completely attached to the child she calls the Misfit Prince. However, it had come at a price. She will have to move six times due to interactions with the police, and Paul had found that fighting is a gift instead of a way to better himself mentally.

Paul liked the adrenaline surge when he draws blood, but there was a time in Ireland that nearly cost Paul his life. When he drew blood, it was from a ten-year-old boy, and things were different. The boy had some sort of virus, and when Paul came in contact with that blood, it made him weaker. His superpower had a super weakness. If he drew blood on a healthy person, he would grow tremendously stronger; however, if the human were sick, or worse, if the human had a virus, it would not just make him ill, it would drain the life out of him, depending on how badly the human was infected. This boy had cancer and drained him so badly that Eileen thought that he was going to die. Paul's skin turned a shade of yellow, and he was peeing blood. Paul's body was trying to heal itself by peeing out the poison. This was how Elaine learned about Tran's gift; Milkies can heal themselves by peeing out the damaged cells out of their bodies.

The problem was, Paul was not a Milky and cannot heal himself the same way. Even though the little gift that Tran gave him makes Paul try to heal himself the same way. For a small virus like a cold, it definitely would work, but this time he found himself in grave danger. He needed a doctor that would not ask too many questions. This is the main reason that Eileen has been moving them from country to country so frequently. Doctors do not want to treat magical humans. Magic goes against everything that doctors are taught. Magic is not science.

Back in the United States, now that Miss Ruby had left, Jeffrey was trying to tell Mary about what happened at the hospital without getting her upset.

Jeffrey walked up to Mary and said, "I need to tell you about a weird thing that happened at the hospital. At the hospital, I'm sure that somebody was watching Susan."

"The car was nothing like I had seen before. The windows were blacked out all the way around, and there were two people in the car. One of them was taking pictures of us. When I noticed them, they stopped. After the nurse and I had Susan in the car, I walked over toward the car, but it sped off." Jeffrey continued. "It gave me cold chills down my spine to know that somebody was watching me or Susan. If you see a car like that, call me and the police."

Mary said, "Why are you trying to scaring me! There are a lot of cars with dark windows! Who would be following you or Susan? We aren't famous…we're nobodies. Besides, what kind of people do you think drive around in a car like that? Mafia? Police? Who do you think it was?"

Jeffrey said, "Maybe I'm just being paranoid, but when I go outside, I feel like we're being watched, and now this car. Maybe I need to go and talk to a shrink about everything."

Mary said, "We don't need to pay somebody to have them say that you lost your only brother and your daughter and that it's okay to grieve. We can't even afford a ramp for Susan's wheelchair, and you want to pay somebody to talk to you? I'll talk to you for free. Luna was my daughter too."

The mysterious black car continued driving around, and it stopped in front of Mark Goldman's house. They had noticed there was a large section of burnt grass by the house. This looked like the place where the Council may have made their entrance. A burnt yard was a sure sign. The two men looked at the area and sensed another Milky. They both got out of their car and started walking to the door. Mark felt the presence of the Milkies walking up and looked out the window. He sensed that they were Milkies but creepy. They had the same black hats and long trench coats with boots. Mark saw them stop and stare at the area that was burnt when the Council arrived. Mark had planted fresh seed in that area, with hopes that it would cover the burnt area. Mark went out to greet the two new Milkies to the area and invited them inside to talk.

After the door was closed, Mark turned around and saw that the two were looking at the floor.

"My name is Terrel Brown, and this is Clinton Black," Terrel said. He continued by saying, "We are pleased to finally reach one of the teams we were assigned to twelve years ago. We have been tracking Paul for over eleven years all over the world ever since the Council announced that they found him near Montréal. We have gotten close several times, and we were on our way back to Canada when we heard about Sean's signal 13. So we made a slight detour to see if we could be of assistance.

Mark smiled and said, "Nice to have more sets of eyes on the O'Neills. I've got a lot to tell you about. First, I'm curious. As I came through the porthole, I lost track of everybody. Where did you land on earth? When you arrived on earth, were you close by each other, or did you find each other along the way?"

Terrel said, "We were sorted nearly together in the middle of a jungle in Brazil. We spent a lot of time helping other Milkies with other Jumpers while following our assignment, always following the weather. If we notice an unusual and very powerful storm, we look for the largest lightning strikes. The Council normally comes in the big storms to see somebody, but the storm that came here had a larger concentration of lightning strikes than I'd ever seen, and by the looks of the crystal floor, I'd say the council member that came was very powerful."

Mark said, "There were seven council members—"

Terrel interrupted him, "Seven! I've never seen more than two and to produce a floor like this. Who were they?"

Mark said, "Malaywah came in person, as well as Oden."

Terrel and Clinton had a surprised look on their face. They had never been this close to two of the most powerful council members. Mark continued, "Malaywah tapped his staff on the floor and changed it to crystal. Since then, Oden has come back through the crystal to warn us of a Milky that has gone rogue. His name is James White, and he is the Georgetown sheriff. He is raging a personal war against the entire O'Neill family. Felicia said we are to protect and guide Sean and that he may be vulnerable."

Clinton interrupted, "Felicia was here also! We have never heard of Felicia ever coming to a debriefing."

Mark said, "Yes."

Clinton said, "If this is any sign of things to come for Sean, we had better not fail him. Terrel and I have stopped at nearly thirty debriefings on the way and had never seen a debriefing that had sent more than one or two council members. Seven were here, including Malaywah?"

Clinton said, "And you are the guard that is running this case? Tell us how we can help. Also, what ability or enhancement was Sean get gifted with after his test?"

Mark responded, "Oden told us that he was not to be enhanced or gifted an ability yet, but just watched for now, and yes, we could use your help. James is the issue we need help with. However, James has not responded well to our mental powers of persuasion. James is going to be a formidable adversary. He has been spending a lot of this time plotting against the O'Neill family, and our powers don't work well on such negative energy. You two are going to have to handle this problem with any means you can."

Mary was standing in the kitchen staring out the window feeling all alone. "Jeffrey has me a little paranoid now," she said to herself.

"Mom," Sean said, trying to get her attention. "I'm going riding."

Mary was still staring out the window thinking about Luna, oblivious to her son, but then she saw him outside riding his bike. "Jeffrey," she called. "Where is Sean going?"

Jeffrey said, "He just told you that he was going for a ride."

Zeke and Zach Mahoney were twins and lived down the street about a mile. Zeke was on the swim team with Sean, and they had been close friends for several years. Sean pulled his bike up at Zeke's house. Kimberly, who was Zeke's little sister and a complete knockout, was sitting on the front porch. Sean invited them to ride bikes down to Pine Tree World.

Pine Tree World was a large ravine deep in the woods that Zach and Zeke found about five years ago. Large cascading trees made it impossible for underbrush to clutter the wooded area, and for kids, this was the perfect place to play and explore. Now as the kids were getting a little older, it was just the perfect place to hang out. It was the end of summer, and the weather was beautiful. After a hard afternoon of playing, there were always plenty of snacks to be found, like blackberries and wild strawberries. This was Sean's favorite place. It was like time stopped here. Cars couldn't get back here, and it was just acres and acres of woods and an enormous pond with a beaver dam that was nearly a half of a mile wide. Not to mention the complete tranquility of nature—the peaceful sound of the birds and always some sort of animals to admire. Everybody came here to watch the beavers or an occasional deer running through the woods. Anybody who has ever seen Pine Tree World has the same thoughts. "If the Creator ever took a vacation, this is where he would go."

Zach was the first out of the house. "Hi, Sean! Pine Tree World? Count me in!" Zeke said, "Me too!" And Kimberly added a loud, "Wait for me!"

They all got on their bikes and started heading for the woods when a car pulled up. Sean looked up and saw that it was his mom.

"Are you trying to give me a heart attack?" Mary asked Sean.

Sean yelled back, "I told you I was going for a ride, we're all going to Pine Tree World."

Mary was trying to put herself into Sean's shoes; she figured that Sean just didn't want to be around the house seeing Susan in her wheelchair. Mary said, "You know what time dinner is, don't be late." Mary was still feeling a little paranoid but said, "Have fun!" and went back home.

Sean and the kids were pumped for some afternoon fun. As they were riding through the woods, they were laughing and joking, anxious to get to their favorite spot. To the kids in the neighborhood, this was a place where adults never came. It was too beautiful for adults, and there were no bedrooms to clean, no lawns to mow, no trash to take out on Tuesdays, and besides, adults would just screw it up with bulldozers, trucks, and cars.

The fresh air of the pine trees and the cherry trees had such an amazing smell to them that all the kids liked to climb them so that their shirts picked up that smell. The beaver dam was at the edge of the area that has been proclaimed Pine Tree World. The trail was well worn from all the kids in the area riding their bikes and breaking any branches from any bushes that got in their way.

Sean and his friends were almost there, and the sight that they all waited for. The beaver dam let them know that they were there. They would always walk on the dam to see if they could make the beavers come out; the best time was in the spring. The beavers were fixing the dam from winter, and the babies were so cute. Everybody had a different idea of what to do once they reached Pine Tree World. Kimberly always wanted to go collect strawberries, Sean and Zeke wanted to cruise their bikes up and down the ravine, and Zach wanted to skip rocks on the beaver pond. Of course, once Zach started skipping rocks, everybody wanted to skip rocks, and once you were skipping rocks, the rest of the world didn't matter. While they were hunting skipping rocks and enjoying life, this was not the only thing going on in the woods.

James was on the prowl for O'Neill blood! He had watched Sean leave the house on his bike, and then saw Mary leave and come back without Sean. There was only one house at the end of that road, the Mahoney house. James made his way quietly through the woods over by the Mahoney house, scouting around with his binoculars. He said to himself, "I'm sure that brat is here somewhere." He noticed that there were no bikes in the yard, and since he had not seen any of the kids on the road, they must've gone there. He saw the bike trail that went into the woods. James had no idea where the trail went after that but thought it couldn't go very far. He carefully and quietly made his way to the trail. After a good long hike, he could hear the sounds of the kids laughing and cutting up. He knew that they couldn't be much farther.

The first one he spotted was Kimberly. Just the sight of such a beautiful girl would make anyone smile. Kimberly could easily be a homecoming queen in a couple years, with dark brown eyes and a smile that would make anybody do whatever she wanted, but James was not just any man. James saw her and smiled. This was the perfect practice shot to warm up his rifle, but good fortune was on Kimberly's side, because he saw the boys, and his eyes went bloodshot red with hate. He steadied himself and was taking aim. "I have you now," he said to himself, thinking of his next few minutes. A stay bullet in the woods will not be too suspicious. Just then, his walkie-talkie squawked, "James, are you there?" It was his buddy, Mike. James lay down on the ground quickly and answered it.

"Kind of busy," James said.

Mike said, "I've been thinking about your problem."

Kimberly came up to James and startled him. "What are you doing, Sheriff?" she asked.

James quickly turned off his walkie-talkie. "I was looking for snakes," James blurted out.

Kimberly said, "There are no snakes here." Kimberly turned into the direction of the boys and yelled, "Hey, guys, the sheriff wants to know if you've seen any snakes."

Just then, another group of kids came up on their bikes. James knew that he didn't have a chance and picked up his rifle. There were just too many kids now. James said, "You kids be careful out here."

"We will, Sheriff," Kimberly said and ran off with the other kids.

James was walking out of the woods on the trail when he saw the black car with blacked-out windows turn around. He had never seen that car in this neighborhood before. It was Terrel and Clinton. They had left Mark's house and located a place to move into that was close by the O'Neill's house. Mark had told them to lookout for the O'Neill family, and they figured the best way was to be their neighbor. There was a house for rent just two doors down and across the street from the side of the O'Neill's house. This place was perfect. It had a great view on two sides of the O'Neill house, plus, as an extra bonus, it sat up a little higher with two stories. They had both unpacked the car and changed into clothes that didn't stand out so much and were just looking around outside the house when Jeffrey looked out the window and saw the black car.

"Mary!" Jeffrey screamed. "It's the black car I saw at the hospital, I know that's got to be it. I'm going to go check it out."

Before Mary could even say anything, Jeffrey was out the door and headed across the yard and toward the two men. Jeffrey was not a big man or an aggressive man, but he was a daddy that had been through a lot of emotional turmoil and his "daddy claws" were out and ready to do business. Jeffrey directly approached the two strangers. "Were you guys taking pictures of me and my daughter at the hospital?"

"I don't know what you are talking about. Who are you?" Terrel said, knowing full well who Jeffrey was, but Jeffery didn't know that.

"I'm Jeffrey O'Neill, and it looked like you guys were at the hospital this morning taking pictures of me and my daughter, and now you're here in front of my house."

Terrel said, "This is our house, and we are in our driveway, not at your house. We had just finished eating breakfast at that little diner right next to the hospital."

Terrel was using his telepathy powers to knock Jeffrey's mind off balance. "We're new in this area, we just found this place to rent, and it seems like a nice little area, or at least we thought it was until now."

Jeffrey started calming down and said, "It looked like you were taking pictures."

Terrel chuckled and said, "Taking pictures of what? The hospital?"

Clinton said, "We are crab fishermen from up in the Baltic Sea. We only work three months of the year, and we were looking for a warmer place to live the other seven months. Thought we'd try this year around here."

Jeffrey smiled a small smile and said, "What's up with the blackened windows on your car?"

Terrel said, "We had that done to the car when we were in California a couple of years ago. The sun's pretty hot and really rough on the inside of a car." Terrel was able to use some of his Milky powers now that Jeffrey was not angry and had Jeffrey go back home with a very comfortable feeling.

Clinton and Terrel were still walking around their house when they both sensed the heat of anger nearby. They both looked at each other and could feel that there was a large concentration of anger very close. Terrel went to go in the house to try to get in contact with Mark. He figured that much heat had to be James, and he could not be far away. Just then, down the street, Clinton noticed a man walking up the road with a rifle and then get into a car and drive past their house.

The heat started to go down after the car drove away. Clinton knew that had to be James and surely the source of anger. The threat to Sean was real. If Sean were going to live long enough to be a Jumper, their job was going to be difficult. Interaction between humans and Milkies normally didn't take place until after the human is sixteen years old and after their HEART test. Clinton was thinking that this was a gray zone. Sean had his test and survived but hadn't received anything. Signal 13 was invoked, and Sean proved himself to be calm under pressure even at a young age. But with the rogue sheriff after him, would he actually make it to sixteen? Clinton knew that this was going to be an assignment that Milkies would talk about for decades.

CHAPTER 8

Terrel and Clinton were well accepted in the neighborhood as summer gave way to fall. There was a crispness in the air as the seasons have changed and school has started back up. Susan and Sean were greeted at the school entrance by Miss Ruby.

Mary was standing at the sidewalk, and she waved to Miss Ruby. Miss Ruby walked out to talk with Mary as the kids made their way to class and said, "How's everything going?"

Mary said, "If the prosthetic works, Susan should be out of the wheelchair…hopefully by Christmas."

Miss Ruby said, "That's wonderful, and how about Sean and Jeffery?"

Mary answered, "Sean's fine, and Jeffrey and I are trying to put the accident behind us. Jeffrey has been talking about having another child, but I think he's still in denial over the loss of Luna. He still won't talk about what happened to her and still changes the subject anytime somebody brings up her name. He has talked himself into believing that if he had been there he may have been able to prevent it."

Miss Ruby said, "We have a new school counselor on staff, and I could have him come over and see you all after school sometime if you'd like. There is no charge to use the school counselor, so you don't have to worry about that."

"I'll mention it to Jeffrey. I'm sure it wouldn't hurt," Mary said.

Miss Ruby looked at her watch. "You have my number, so call me if we can help, but it looks like I need to get to class." Miss Ruby walked away thinking to herself that just because it's been quiet for the last month, doesn't mean the family was still not in danger.

Martha was thinking that the reason Jeffrey was actually thinking about having another child was to forget about what happened over the summer, but she knew that the O'Neill drama was not over. If certain people found out, this could spur on new attacks on the family. She thought she had better call Mark and keep him informed about Mary and Jeffrey and the possibilities of a baby.

The Council was making its rounds going from case to case in the area. The Milkies always knew that the Council could show up at any time and that the Council was undetectable by anyone. Some of the council members move Milkies around if they think that a Jumper needs different help, and Clinton knew that there was a chance that other Milkies would show up. He was right. About a month ago, there was a Milky by the name of Robert Rose. Mark was happy to have another Milky find his way to help with Sean. Robert's cover as school psychologist was an easy fit; he was a mere five foot one inch tall and very thin in stature, totally not threatening in appearance to anyone.

Martha got on the intercom and summoned Robert Rose to her office. When he arrived, Robert saw a troubled look on Martha's face.

"Robert," Martha said, "I'm going to arrange for you to pay a visit to the O'Neill house. Sean's handling everything fine, but Mr. O'Neill's mental state could affect Sean. I'm worried about Sean, and we need him to stay focused for as long as we can. I think that we will be told to give Sean another HEART test when he turns sixteen. I'm guessing. A HEART test at twelve is not normal, so a second HEART test is not out of the question. I just hope that Sean starts developing his ability, which would help make everybody's life more relaxed."

A knock on the door interrupted the meeting. It was Mr. Knickerbocker, Sean's history teacher. "I'm sorry to interrupt, but we have a problem that you need to take care of." He had two boys with him, Sean O'Neill with bloody lip and Brian Bass the class bully. Every school and every grade everywhere has one.

Miss Ruby said, "This school year has barely started. Do you mind telling me what is going on?"

Sean sat there quietly while Brian blurted out, "He started it!

"Did not!" Sean said.

"One at a time! Sean, what's going on?"

"I was just talking to Zeke about my dad and mom wanting to have another baby, and Brian came over and punched me in the mouth."

Brian said, "My dad said that the O'Neills were nothing but a bunch of cockroaches, and when he was bragging about getting to have a little brother, well, I just got mad that there was going to be another one."

Miss Ruby said, "The O'Neills are not cockroaches. They are good people just like you, and I will speak to your father about this. Sean, I want you to go back to classroom, and Brian, you go wait out in the hallway. I'm going to call your father." Miss Ruby tried to compose herself, wondering how she could ever accustom herself to these human emotions. Anger is such a strong emotion that humans have so easy.

Brian's father came to the school. A foul odor preceded him as he came into the school—a mix of body odor and something else. His eyes were completely bloodshot red.

Brian's father stood in the front office and announced himself, "I am Mike Bass. I was told I needed to come in and see Miss Ruby about my son. I was told that my boy was in a fight here in school." Mike looked down the hallway and saw his son sitting in a chair. "Boy!" Mike bellowed. "Who did you get in a fight with now?"

Miss Ruby interrupted Mr. Bass, "Mr. Bass, please come in and sit down."

The two of them made their way into her office. Mike leaned over toward Miss Ruby, and with a foul smell coming out of his mouth said, "You can call me Mike, all the women call me Mike."

A woman would have to be desperate to even get close enough to you with a stench like you have, Miss Ruby thought to herself and then walked back to her chair.

Miss Ruby sat in her chair. "Mr. Bass, please sit down. I called you in here because your son punched another boy in the mouth, and he thinks that his behavior is what you want him to do. He also said that the boy's whole family was nothing but a bunch of cockroaches."

Mike Bass's body language after hearing the story told Miss Ruby immediately; this man is James White's new best friend.

"Let me guess," Mike said, "it was one of those worthless O'Neill kids?"

Martha sat squirming in her chair about how hateful this human is.

Mike continued, "That truck should have taken out all three of those kids and the mama."

Martha's hands were below the desk, and they started to glow. The ability to incinerate with their hands is the most powerful weapon that a Milky possess. She had to calm herself down. If she grabbed him as infuriated as she was becoming, her hands could turn him to cinders. Martha said in a calm manner, "You need an attitude change and to stop poisoning your boy with your opinions." Martha continued to squirm in her seat, just itching to get rid of this evil in front of her. However, there are strict guidelines about evil, and this guy drips of evil. "Brian is suspended from school for three days. Take him home, and he better come back with a different attitude about the O'Neills. Every human is important, and the O'Neill family is no exception."

Mike said, "Nothing will change the way I feel about them. You ought to kick the whole family out of this school before they poison any of the other kids." Mike got up and walked out of Martha's office and beckoned for Brian to come with him. He smiled at Brian and told him, "You didn't do anything wrong except that you got caught." The two of them headed out the door.

Martha sat down and took a drink of her sweet tea, trying to calm down from her close encounter with pure evil. Martha then called Mary O'Neill on the phone.

"Hello, Mary, this is Miss Ruby from school. Your son had an incident here at the school today, and I need to talk to you about it. Sean got in a little fight today. It was not his fault, but I am worried about him. I know we just spoke about Mr. Rose coming to speak with Jeffrey, but I believe that the whole family should be there. After what just happened, Sean should also speak with him. It is up to you."

THE COMMON MAN

Mary said, "Is he okay? What happened?"

"He's fine, he's got a little bloody lip, but he's fine. One of the other boys was a little jealous about Sean and that he may be getting a new baby brother or sister."

"I don't understand," Mary said.

"Please let Mr. Rose come over in the evening and talk with you all. He's the new school counselor that I was telling you about."

"I'll talk to Jeffrey and get back with you. I think that would be fine, but I needed to talk to my husband first."

"I understand," Miss Ruby said. "Please call me back and let me know."

Miss Ruby got off the phone and then picked up the phone again and called Mark. "Mark, we have a new problem. We need to get everybody together. We had a situation at school today that everybody on this case needs to know about."

Mark said, "I'll call everybody, and we will meet at my house tonight at eight o'clock."

"Oh, Canada," Eileen was singing to herself as she was walking through the airport in Montréal for the third time with Paul and Tran. This time would be different; Eileen contacted the Council that she and Tran were back in Canada and not on a case. This time they moved, not because Tran had killed someone but because Tran incited a riot in Japan to "teach Paul how to influence a large crowd."

This is what Japan called an unprovoked domestic attack by outside forces. Meaning they had no idea what caused such a large riot. The newspaper had blurry images of Tran dragging a man down the street. Eileen just wanted to separate Tran from Paul. She was outstanding at her job, and Paul was excelling in multiple languages thanks to her interactions. However, spending so much contact time with a human has brought out some motherly emotions. Eileen had watched the daily bruises and washed the bloody clothing for years. She had to separate them but had not come up with a game plan yet.

She just knew she had to separate them, or Paul's future would be permanently set in stone. Eileen was thinking of a plan, how to separate Paul from Tran, but that wasn't the problem that was looming in her mind. It was the thought of going against the powerful

Zimbabwe. She figured that if she could get Paul to draw enough blood from Tran, he would be weak enough for her to overpower him, but still, how can she explain this to Zimbabwe? Eileen had done many cases over the decades for Zimbabwe, but she had never considered going against Zimbabwe's directions. With so much contact time with a human, Eileen had started to develop mama bear emotions, and after caring for Paul for so long, she was ready for her claws to come out.

There was so much chatter on Mark's phone to all the other Milkies in the area that the Council was aware that something was going on. This was the first time that everybody on the Sean O'Neill case had gotten together. When Robert walked in, he noticed the crystal floor, and other Milkies kept coming to the house.

Robert said, "This is no average Jumper case, is this? I've never seen a crystal floor before."

Mark said, "Malaywah himself tapped his staff on the floor, and it turned into a crystal porthole for them to travel unnoticed."

Terrel and Clinton were already at the house when Martha showed up thinking she was last as they all went in to go sit down at the table. Mark went to sit at the head of the table when the crystal shook, and a cloud appeared. It was Felicia from the Council. Mark dropped to one knee and acknowledged Felicia and then offered the seat at the head of the table, as they all acknowledged Felicia's power.

Felicia said, "Continue. I am just here to observe in person."

Martha said, "I called everybody here to inform you that the entire O'Neill family may be in danger. Today at school, one of the boys in Sean's class picked a fight with him because his father told him that his entire family was nothing but a bunch of cockroaches, and upon confronting the father, things got worse. The father said that it was a shame that the truck didn't eliminate all three kids and the mama."

Everybody was muttering among each other. Mark asked, "Was this James?"

"No," Martha said, "but he's made himself one of James's closest friends. His name is Mike Bass. He's an unproductive human with a drug addiction, and his hatred is rubbing off on his son."

Clinton says, "Our powers of persuasion are useless against hate, and the stronger the hate, the less we're able to see around humans."

Felicia could tell that all the guards were nervous and knew that protocol would not allow for them to just eliminate evil.

Felicia said, "Evil is part of the equation. Sean is our main concern. Malaywah made it clear that we are to protect Sean and help steer him onto a better path for his future. That does not mean that we are to eliminate all the evil that Sean comes in contact with. However, if it comes to be that Sean is in immediate danger, then and only then, take whatever actions necessary. Sean's family is not our concern unless he is targeted also." Felicia stood up and spoke one more time, "Sean is your focus. That rest of the family is not our concern." Felicia stepped away from the table, and then just as quickly as she came, she faded into a cloud and then into the crystal floor.

Mark said, "Terrel, you and Clinton keep an eye on the O'Neill house. Robert, try to watch out for James and find out if he has any plans against Sean." Mark continued, "I wish they would just go ahead and give Sean his enhancement as a Jumper, whatever the enhancement. Our path would definitely be easier than the path we are following now."

Clinton said, "Next time one of the council members shows up…why don't we just ask them?"

Mark said, "I'm not going to question Oden. I have said that before, and I'll say it again, I'm not going to end up as a pile of dust."

Martha said, "The weather will be changing soon, and the cold makes the humans even more unpredictable." Martha was looking at Mark and addressed him, "You're the lead on this case and the only one who can use the radio radar. It would be great if you could locate a couple more Milkies to help at the dead end behind the O'Neill house."

Mark closed his eyes and, using his powers as lead, started searching for any newcomers in the area. Mark started pointing to the north and said, "Two guards just showed up on the radar near Montreal, neither one of them appear to be on a case. I'll see if I can get them from their area and get them on this case. That's strange! They don't seem to be responding to my signal. I'll take a trip to Canada to find out for sure and also to see what cases they have worked. I'll leave tomorrow morning. If anything happens, call Martha. She will have access to my house, and if you all need to meet, do it at my house. My house is the only one with the crystal floor, and if the Council needs to come, the crystal floor is the quickest porthole."

Martha said, "Robert, don't forget tomorrow night you have an appointment at the O'Neill's house to talk to Jeffrey and check on Sean."

Mike and James were drinking at the Over the Top Beer Hub when Mike said, "One of those O'Neill cockroaches got my boy kicked out of school for three days and all he did was punch him in the mouth."

James responded, "What are you talking about?"

"My Brian overheard the O'Neill boy saying that his mom and dad maybe having another baby, so Brian punched him in the mouth."

James spouted out, "You mean to tell me that there may be another O'Neill coming?"

If smoke could come out of a human's ears when they were going to blow their top, James's ears would be blowing smoke.

James took another guzzle of his beer. "We have got to come up with a plan to where we have a perfect alibi. First thing is we can't let another O'Neill come into this world, no more cockroaches."

"How about this," Mike said. "Once we see them all go to sleep, we could just go ahead and blow the whole house up once they are sleeping."

James looked at Mike with a dumb look, "Real smart, Mike! The feds would swarm this place, and you would be a primary suspect because your boy got in a fight with Sean. Now, don't misunderstand me. I'm not saying an explosion would be a bad thing but… wait a minute. What if we were all at a hunting camp way over in Kentucky when the explosion happened? We could gas the house at night. That would knock them all out, and then get one of those timers from the hardware store and set it for like, eight hours.

"That's brilliant," Mike said, "but where do we get the gas?"

James said, "Leave that to me. The evidence locker is like an invisible candy store full of good stuff. The locker is at the police department. If I find something we can use, I'm sure there's other things that I can move around and then it will be just written off as missing."

"What the hell you looking at?" James blurted out, talking to a woman three tables over.

Mike turned around.

James was talking with his teeth locked together. "That bitch keeps staring at me with those funky eyes."

Mike started laughing.

Both one of them were under the influence of LSD mixed with alcohol. Mike tried to talk, but he couldn't stop laughing at James. "That LSD must be good, because not only do I not see any girl over there, but there isn't anybody at that table." Mike kept laughing because he could see how mad James was getting.

James said, "The one right there with the funky eyes."

It was Felicia. She was only making herself visible to test James. She could feel the heat from the hate. A Milky could sense two things stronger than anything else, hate and fear. Fear was different—fear emotions were extreme cold. Felicia wanted to turn the two of them to dust but knew she couldn't eliminate evil from the equation. All she could do was watch helplessly and wait for things to unfold. Felicia was hoping that she could make them both paranoid enough that they would leave, or hopefully, the paths that they were taking would change. Unfortunately, a Milky had no ability to alter the thought process of hate. She watched and studied these two humans as they indulged in alcohol and mind-altering drugs, and that maybe making them see ghosts, then maybe, just maybe, they might alter their plans. It was an untested idea, but if she could change their thoughts from hate to fear, then maybe this threat to Sean would subside, and he would make it to his next HEART test at sixteen years old. Felicia made her eyes get bigger, staring at him as if she was touching his soul with her eyes. James's facial expression started to change.

Bam!

Mike punched James in the face, knocking him to the floor.

Mike was laughing so hard, he could hardly talk, "There, did you see that?"

"All right, you two," the bartender yelled. "No fighting in here, both of you outside before I call the cops."

James was lying on the floor laughing and yelled at the bartender, pulling out his badge and gun, "I am the cops."

They both waived off the bartender and headed outside. Felicia knew that this wasn't the end. Malaywah was correct; you can't do away with evil. The humans have to deal with it themselves.

Mark arrived in Montréal in search of the two Milkies that showed up on radar as new in the area. Mark headed out to a remote area just outside of town, knowing they wouldn't be far from there. Mark was like a bloodhound following a distinct scent even in the snow. Mark started toward the house when a black car pulled up. It was Tran. Tran got out of the car and made his hands in the shape of a circle. His hands started to glow through his gloves. Tran has always been one of those no-nonsense, no playing, and no kidding around kind of badasses.

Mark said, "Wait! I am the leader of the Sean O'Neill case. I've come to see if you…"

Tran interrupted him and said, "You are not authorized to be near Paul."

"No!" Mark said. "That's not why I'm here. I've come here to see if you could help us with the Sean O'Neill case." Mark walked up a little closer, and Tran quickly rotated his glowing hands into Mark's chest, turning him to dust. Mark had unknowingly encountered Zimbabwe's problem solver, a mistake that he never saw coming.

CHAPTER 9

A week has passed, and Martha was starting to wonder when Mark would return. Martha called Robert into her office. "I haven't heard from you in a week about your meeting with the O'Neill family. Care to share?"

Robert said, "Jeffrey has been working late, but we are set to meet this Friday. Any word from Mark?"

"Not a word," Martha said. "In fact, since he has been gone, he hasn't even called, and Terrel and Clint told me that they haven't seen anything happening around the O'Neill house. It's been strangely quiet. I think we all need to get together after your meeting with the O'Neill's at Mark's house."

It was Friday night, and Robert was on his way to meet up with the O'Neill family. When Robert arrived at the O'Neill house, Clinton was watching the back of the house and Terrel was focusing on the front of the house. Robert walked up to the front door and was greeted by Mary. Robert shook hands with Jeffrey and said hello to Susan and Sean. When Sean touched Robert's hand, it was like electricity.

Puberty! This is the time when all Jumpers start to develop their ability, which, of course, is the purpose of the HEART test, to see if a young Jumper is worthy of keeping his ability and also getting an enhancement to their ability.

Robert's eyes lit up, and it seemed that Sean was looking through his eyes. Sean was developing powers of transfer. The Milkies were worried that he would develop this power after they'd witnessed him holding onto Paul at the sorting table. Robert pulled his hand away and tried to play it off by laughing and said, "You...you...you shocked me, Sean," as if he had had a static electrical charge hit him. Robert was stuttering from the jolt.

Sean said, "I could see you looking at me."

Robert was not ready for that or knew the right way to respond. Robert's body felt tingly.

Jeffrey said, "We have plenty of room to sit around the dining room table, if that's okay with you, Mr. Rose."

Robert tried hard to concentrate on being a psychologist, but Sean would not take his eyes off of him.

Robert knew that Sean's powers depended on how long he had held on to Paul at the sorting table. Robert stuttered again, "I guess that's fine."

Mary said, "I guess that's fine." Mary took offense to that thinking, *What's the matter with my dining room table?*

Her voice brought Robert back. "I'm sorry, Mary, I didn't hear you."

Mary repeated what Jeffery said, "Do you want to sit at the dining room?"

Robert said, "Yes, yes, that will be great."

Mary said, "My scars are starting to heal pretty slowly, but I guess that's normal."

"Yes," Robert said, "We heal faster on the outside than the inside. It takes a long time to forgive, but you will probably never forget."

After an hour of speaking with the family and counseling, Robert said, "Time is slipping away. Hard to believe I've…I've…I've been here so long." He was starting to stutter again because of Sean. Sean was standing right next to him. Robert got up and started to the door and stopped at Susan. He bent down so that he could look Susan in the eye and told her things would get better. Looking into her eyes, Robert was trying to use his powers of persuasion, but nothing would happen. At the same time, Sean came over and touched Robert's hand. Sean was absorbing some of his powers.

Robert pulled his hand away and tried to play it off again, "You…you…you shocked me again."

Sean just looked at him. He could feel the energy that he just received.

Robert knew he had to get out of there, say something, and stop stuttering. Robert stood up and said, "I need to go," and headed to the door.

Sean looked up at Robert and said, "Mr. Rose, who is the Council?"

The rest of family had a strange look on their faces because Robert didn't say anything out loud, but Sean had heard his thoughts.

Robert replied, "I'm not sure what you are talking about, Sean," and started walking to the front door. Robert knew that Sean was absorbing his powers the longer that he stayed there. After he was outside, he turned around and said, "If you ever need someone to talk to…y'all know you can call me anytime." With that, Robert left.

Robert was in a hurry to get home so that he could give Martha a call and update about the visit. He started rambling to himself, "A human that can actually transfer powers! This is amazing. Sean was able to see what I was seeing and hear my thoughts without me saying anything. Amazing!"

Robert was driving down the road and almost to his house when he felt the heat, the soul-burning heat that can only come from absolute hate. It was getting stronger as another car was approaching from the other direction. Then the car passed, the burning let up. Robert said to himself, "Sean absorbed some of my powers, but I certainly felt that. I guess he's able to use my powers in my presence. I wonder how strong his powers will get when he goes to school tomorrow. Sean will be in the close vicinity of at least two Milkies."

Robert arrived at his house and ran inside to call Martha. "Martha, everybody needs to meet," he blurted. "Hello! I just left the O'Neill house, and this is something that everybody needs to hear." Robert continued to ramble faster and faster. Finally raising his voice, he almost yelled, "Sean! He is *amazing*! Come now!"

Martha said, "I'll call everybody, and we will all meet at Mark's house tonight." Martha sent out the calls and told everybody to meet at Mark's house. Martha arrived first in the house. It had a glow inside as if somebody were home. Martha said to herself, "Mark didn't tell me that he was back at home."

Just then, Terrel and Clinton pulled up, and Robert was just behind them. They all went up to the door, and when they went inside, Felicia was sitting at the table waiting for them. They all acknowledged Felicia and then took their seats at the table.

Felicia started by saying, "A lot has transpired in the last few days. Your team leader Mark has fallen off the radar and is missing. As you are all aware, the average Jumper case has one or two Milkies assigned to it. This case was assigned thirty, and it takes time for the guards to find their way. Don't go looking for other guards. Just as you found your way here, others are still searching for you and will find their way to you. There are dangers out there that you all are not aware of. With saying that, Martha, you have the helm alone."

Martha says, "Dangers? Who would…I have never encountered…are any of us in danger?"

Felicia said, "Focus on your case. It is not uncommon for a Milky to come up missing. Over the past few years, we've had several guards go missing."

Everyone looked at each other. Martha asked, "Does Paul have something to do with this? You know, the one that came in contact with Sean?" This was a name that they had heard already once before by Malaywah. "Malaywah said that we should prevent Paul and Sean's paths from crossing."

Felicia said, "Just follow your case!"

Robert spoke, "I met with the entire O'Neill family tonight, and we are definitely going to have to deal with a new revelation. Sean is developing transfer powers."

Clinton and Terrel looked at each other. "Is this even possible for a human, you know, to have transfer powers? That is, without the council gifting that human?"

Robert said, "When Sean touched my hand, he was able to see what I see. He was looking at himself through my eyes."

Felicia said, "It has been a long time since we've had a human that has developed transfer powers, and for him to start developing them at only twelve years old certainly justifies the invoking the signal 13. We knew the possibility was there for him to develop some sort of powers because of his extended contact at the sorting table. We can only guess as to how powerful his powers will come to be… if…he were to come in contact with Paul."

Robert said, "His powers are still getting stronger when he is in close proximity to us. I was comforting Susan with my powers of persuasion when Sean touched me again, and this time he was able to read my thoughts. I was looking at him and said to myself that the Council would need to know about this, and Sean said, 'Who is the Council?'"

Felicia said, "This is remarkable. I don't recall another human to be able to absorb the powers of others and use them. I will have to bring this up at the next full Council."

Felicia continued, "On a separate note…just the other day, I felt the tremendous amount of heat from hate. I decided to follow it to a bar and found two people so full of darkness and hate that I decided to try something different. I interacted with one by trying to heighten the emotion of fear to offset the emotion of hate that was so overwhelming with them. From what I saw, fear is a much stronger motion then hate. I realize over the centuries that humans have called us many things, from demons and everything in between to guardian angels. It all depends on whether we are helping them or we're scaring the hell out of them. The council would like you all to try to do the same if you see a situation similar. But until Sean's ability is developed, do not use your powers around him. Malaywah has not said anything about creating a czar. You all will be very restricted on the use of your powers, especially in the proximity Sean. The development of his powers at such a young age could become very dangerous."

Robert interjected, "There something else. I think the contact did more to Sean than we imagined. When he touched me, he was not only absorbing my powers, but it was almost like he was draining the life out of me because I couldn't talk. I stuttered and couldn't clearly make sentences."

Felicia responded, "Unless, only unless, necessary, any Milkies are around Sean are to suppress their powers for several hours to prevent him from absorbing anymore, and let this charge wear off fully. Mind your distance but stay vigilant."

It was now November, and the weather was getting colder.

James called Mike. "It's time," he said.

Mike responded, "Time? You haven't called me in forever and now you tell me it's time…time for what?

"Just come over to my house, and I'll explain everything."

Mike arrived at James's place, and James was outside waiting for him.

James said, "We have some dynamite in the evidence locker, and I know how I will make it disappear. That is not even the good part. I have a whole bottle of nitrous oxide from the hospital."

Mike said, "Now you're speaking my language. When can we play?"

James responded, "It's supposed to start snowing soon, so before it starts, this is the perfect time. The fresh snow will cover up our tracks, and then when the timer goes off, we will be a couple of states away."

"Oh yeah, definitely count me in," said Mike.

James was trying to mask his excitement and calmly said, "The gas will knock the whole family out, and then we'll go in and turn the gas stove on and blow out the flame. Just in case there is not enough gas in the lines to do the job right, I have two sticks of dynamite to do the job."

Mike was laughing with such excitement that he was going to get to play with dynamite that he wet his pants.

James blurted out, "Damn it, Mike, I swear you should be wearing a diaper."

Mike was still laughing and said, "Let me do something. I will not let you down."

James said, "Okay, but first you need to change your pants, you smell like piss. I'll meet you tonight at the edge of the woods behind their house. I first have to get the dynamite."

Jeffrey came home. Mary and Susan were in the kitchen. "What's for dinner?" Jeffrey asked.

Susan said, "We're having Italian tonight, lasagna."

THE COMMON MAN

Sean came into the kitchen. "Can I go to Zeke's house?"

Jeffrey answers, "We're about to have dinner. Did you get all your homework done?"

"Yes. Can I go now?"

"After dinner," Jeffrey said.

Sean was pleading his case, "Mr. Mahoney is making an ice-skating rink behind their house."

"That's great, but you still have to wait till after dinner to go," Jeffrey said.

As the O'Neills were eating, there was something evil going on outside their window. It was dark, and the snow started to fall. Mike and James were fumbling in the woods, trying to get a heavy bottle of nitrous oxide to the backside of the house without making too much noise.

Clinton was sitting on his porch watching the snow and looking in the direction of the O'Neill house. Something caught his eye; he noticed the movement back of their house and decided he needed to take a closer look. Clinton remembered that he was not supposed to use his power so close to Sean, but he could feel the heat from the hate and knew evil was close by. Clinton was sure that he saw two shadows and figured that they were probably up to no good, but he had no idea how much "no good" they were up to.

Different things were going through Clinton's mind: *First and foremost, don't get seen by the O'Neills because I don't want to try to explain why I sneaking around their house.* The main thing was that if he recognized that it was James, to make him go away and try not to use any powers. Even though it was cold outside, the unmistakable heat of hate he was feeling was very strong as he peeked around the corner of the house. He could see one person doing something under the house, but he was sure he saw two people. Just then…bam! Then a whole barrage of hard hits. James snuck up on Clinton and cold-cocked him with the butt of his gun and then beat him unconscious. Mike heard the thuds, turned round, and saw James over the top of a man. Clinton was out cold as blood dripped around the side of his face. James hit him so many times that his right eye was nearly falling out of the socket. James dragged the man around back and whispered to Mike, "Son of a bitch was sneaking up on us. Do you think he is one of those O'Neills?"

Mike said, "I've never seen him before."

James was trying to catch his breath and said, "Doesn't matter. We will put him in the house after we knock them all out, it will look like he broke in."

Just then, he heard the front door close and saw Sean riding his bike away.

"I can't believe this," James erupted. Still trying to remain as quiet as possible, every vein in his neck and his forehead were bulging out, quietly muttering every obscenity that he could possibly think of. "Every time I get it right, something goes wrong."

Mike was looking at James with a dumb look on his face, and then he erupted into a quiet laughter and said, "Come on, we will wait for him to come home in the woods and then will be able to finish the job. Grab the other end of this guy, and we will bring him to the woods." They picked up Clinton and put him in the woods and sat there waiting for Sean to come home.

Clinton had left his house without saying anything to Terrel. Clinton had been gone for about an hour when Terrel noticed him missing.

Terrel was wondering where Clinton went. He could feel that something was wrong, but because Clinton was unconscious, Terrel couldn't figure out why he couldn't sense Clinton's presence. Terrel went outside and started looking around; the air was full of hate! Terrel tilted his head back and breathed in a deep breath. Nothing, no traces of Clinton, just hate. One thing was for sure, the heat of hate was close.

Terrel was thinking, *Something's wrong, something's really wrong. Clinton doesn't just disappear. We've been watching this house for months, and I've always been able to feel Clinton's presence. I don't feel it now.*

Terrel was wondering if he should go in and call for help from Martha or Robert, but if he couldn't feel Clinton's presence, they would not feel his presence either. He figured that he should try to find Clinton the same way that the humans try to find one another.

As the snow began to fall heavier, Terrel yelled, "Clinton!"

Nothing, no response. Terrel walked around his house and walked the road past the O'Neills. By now the snow had covered any tracks or traces of anyone except himself walking around. Something was wrong, really wrong. He had a bad thought come to his head, *Maybe…I don't know…* He was trying to not finish that terrible thought. Clinton couldn't have just disappeared. Terrel now was worried for himself. He had to get help. Terrel ran for his car, completely forgetting that he could've just made a simple phone call for help; instead, he got in and headed for Martha's house.

A couple of hours passed, and the Mahoneys finished building the hockey ring in their backyard. Heavy snow didn't slow Mr. Mahoney down; he was a great carpenter, forming the hockey ring with four-by-four boards then plastic all over the boards and the grass. "There," he said. "That will be a nice hockey ring in the morning!" Mr. Mahoney and the kids watched it filling up with water from a hose.

Sean idolized Mr. Mahoney and wanted to be just like him when he grew up, not to mention the fact that he was crazy about Kimberly and would much rather been at their house than his own house.

"I think it is time for you to go home," Mr. Mahoney said to Sean. "Your mom probably has dinner ready by now."

Sean smiled and wanted to say he already ate. But no words would come out; instead, his brain was wishing Mr. Mahoney would have said, "Do you want to stay for dinner? I can call your mom for you?" But that never happened! Sean felt he was invisible to everyone; the Mahoneys were no different.

Sean simply said, "Okay," and headed home.

The snow was coming down so beautifully. Instead of going into the house, he decided to go around the back of the house and make snow angels. Big puffy snowflakes were perfect for making snowmen and snow angels. Sean thought that when the lights came on, the snow angels would be cool to look at from his bedroom window. Sean lay down in the snow and started making an angel. James and Mike at the wood line were watching like a couple of hungry wolves. James decided this was too easy and started toward Sean.

Terrel had arrived at Martha's house over an hour ago and was waiting for Martha to get home. Terrel noticed a light come on and realized that she had been home the entire time. Terrel got out of his car and started running toward the door when a bright bolt of lightning and a loud boom hit the ground just ahead of him. Martha ran to the door and opened the door. She saw Terrel kneeling and then saw Oden. Martha dropped to one knee.

Oden said, "You are all about to lose your Jumper, Sean! Nobody is watching him, and he is in grave danger."

Terrel said, "Clinton is missing."

Before he could say anything else, Oden said, "Clinton is not your concern. Both of you get over to the O'Neill house and protect your Jumper."

James was almost to Sean. He had the butt end of his gun up in the air and swung it toward Sean's head. Just before the blow arrived, Sean felt James's thoughts and moved, but it wasn't fast enough. The butt of the gun did its job, and Sean la there, bleeding and not making a sound. James had split Sean's head open and knocked him out. The cold air kept the gash from bleeding faster. James thought with a hit like that, and Sean being so young, that Sean would be out for a while. James went back to the woods to help Mike get Clinton from the woods and back to the house. Mike smacked both Clinton and Sean a couple extra times just to make sure they didn't wake up.

Mike went back to work under the house, using a hand drill to drill holes in the floor so that he could insert two plastic tubes to the inside of the house to the manifold at the gas tank and the other to a propane tank. Mike signaled to James, "James, just turn on the nitrous oxide tank slowly."

It was just a matter of time now for the gas to empty into the house. With that much nitrous oxide, they would all drop like flies. Mike was looking in one of the windows, and he could see all three of the O'Neills in the living room watching TV.

"It's working," Mike said. "Damn, that girl is ugly. James, who do you think will drop first?"

James answered, "I hope it is the father. He is probably the only one who might be able to fight it for a while."

Mike said, "The girl's head just fell down, and the Mama is having a hard time keeping her eyes open."

"The dad knows something's up," Mike blurted out. "The mama's down! The mama fell down, and the dad's gagging. It looks like he's making a run for the door. Jeffrey is heading for the door but couldn't get it open, and he's down."

"We got them all! I can't believe that they all fell in under twenty minutes." Mike was squirming like a little girl and could hardly control his laughter. He screamed quietly, "We got them all, we got them all!"

James said, "Good! Throw that guy over your shoulder and put him in the house. I'll grab the boy. Make sure you put your gas mask on before you go in and pull that door close after we are in. I want the gas to stay in for hours. I want to hear in the radio that there was an explosion when we are in Kentucky."

Sean was coming to. His head was hurting. Something terrible was happening! He saw someone carrying a man over his shoulder and knew he was probably next. Sean started to moan, and James came over and grabbed Sean by the coat, picked him up, looked him in the eye, and said, "Why don't you die? Any other kid would have died with a hit in the head like that, but no, you have to live. Don't worry…you will be dead with the rest of your family very soon. You're the cause of this entire mess, you and all the rest of your cockroach O'Neill family." James smacked Sean with the butt of his gun again, knocking him out again. "Damn, you must have the hardest head to take a beating like that and keep waking up." James picked Sean up by his belt and followed Mike to the front of the house.

James and Mike put their masks on and went into the house.

With the gas mask on, James's speech was muffled. "You can die in the house like the rest of your family," he said as he dropped Sean on the floor.

Mike then threw Clinton on the floor next to Sean.

The drop on the floor was like a wake-up button to Sean. He started flailing like an injured dog, but he was hurting too bad to try hard to do anything but moan in agony.

James called to Mike. "Would you look at this kid," he said as Sean continued to flail around on the floor. "He just will not stay down!"

Mike said, "Do you want me to beat him a little more? I don't mind, I kind of enjoy it!"

James said, "I think he just needs another good kick in the head! It's my turn. Boy, I'm going to use your head as a football."

Sean's face went from scared to mad when he saw his family lying on the floor. Clinton was starting to move a little and opened one eye and could see Sean trying to fight for his life. Clinton struggled to reach one hand and grabbed Sean's leg and passed as much life as he could into Sean. Sean could feel the heat from inside him building up his hands. Sean could feel power like he had never felt before surging through his hands. Clinton knew that he was nearly dead, and as a dying gift to humanity, and knowing that without a little help, Sean was about to die, Clinton passed his Milky powers to Sean, gifting Sean with all his abilities. This would be considered the ultimate sacrifice of a Milky.

Sean's hands started to smoke and were getting hot.

James noticed the heat coming from Sean and kicked Sean in the back as he tried to crawl on the floor.

"You freak!" James said.

Sean grabbed James by the leg, and James screamed with agony as Sean transferred the heat from his hands directly onto James's leg, giving him instant paralysis and catching his pants and his leg on fire. Sean kept holding onto James's pants, and the fire got hotter and hotter. James was screaming in agony! James's entire body stiffened like a board and fell to the floor.

Mike, upon seeing what was happening to James, ran out the door like the little weasel that he was. With the door open, the fire was acting like a giant vacuum, sucking in the much-needed air, fueling the fire and causing the fire to grow. With the fire burning, it was also mixing fresh air with the gas, forcing the gas to escape from the house. Sean's family was not dead yet; the gas just knocked them out. Thanks to the fire, they started coming to. As James was smoldering in the middle of the floor, the fire started to spread throughout the living room. The fire was a two-edged sword; it was forcing fresh air in making the room breathable, but now the house was catching on fire.

Jeffrey started coughing and then Mary. They started to come back to life, fighting to live with every cough.

The effect of the gas was quickly burning off, but now the smoke from the fire was starting to take a toll. Their bodies were coughing, trying to force the gas out of their bodies, but now it was being replaced with smoke, making them cough even harder.

Sean was trying to yell, "Dad! Mom! Fire!" Nothing but a painful squeak. Sean may have killed James, but the damage that James had done to him first made Sean unable to talk or get himself out of the fire.

Jeffrey was rolling slowly on the floor, gagging for air. Jeffrey was trying to stagger to his feet because he was close to the door but still heavily under the effects of the gas and the knock on the head from hitting the door and now gagging on smoke. Jeffrey dropped to his knees on the porch.

Mary also started coughing for fresh air; she started to crawl across the floor, eyeing the door. Finally to the door, she was gagging for fresh air on the porch.

"The kids, Jeffrey!" Mary yelled. "Get Susan, she's dying.

Jeffrey staggered to his feet, trying to find Susan in the thick smoke.

Jeffrey saw Susan slumped over in the chair. "Susan! Wake up, Susan!"

Jeffrey made his way inside. The fire was spreading fast throughout the house. He staggered over to her chair and, as quickly as he could, rolled her outside. Jeffery was rushing to the door, seeing his house burn. He thought he saw Sean as he got Susan out on the porch. Jeffrey looked in as the fire was now licking the ceiling and could see Sean lying on the floor. Sean was bleeding on the floor, trying to crawl but going nowhere.

The fire was growing by the minute; Jeffery went back in. Jeffrey's eyes, fixed on the burned image of a man on the floor next to Sean, grabbed Sean, and the two of them struggled to get outside.

Just then, an enormous explosion!

The fire had finally burned through where the hoses were pumping gas into the house, reaching the gas bottle behind the house. And when that explosion went off, it detonated the sticks of dynamite that James had in the backyard, causing the second massive explosion. The explosion was so large that it blew a crater in the backyard.

The explosion had one benefit; it was so strong that it actually blew the fire out.

Martha and Terrel were almost to the house when they saw the explosion. They thought they failed; no one could have survived that explosion. They pulled up as close to the house as they could get. Pieces of the house were raining down everywhere.

They could sense that someone was still alive but where? A Milky could only sense other Milkies; they had no ability to sense ordinary humans, so who was in the pile? What other Milky could have been at the house? They knew they had to find the person that they sensed. They followed their senses, pulling boards and pieces of the house, personal belongings all blown apart, and then…a foot, a leg, there had to be more. Terrel lifted some boards and saw that it was Susan, and she was alive. The explosion blew Susan in her wheelchair off the porch, and her wheelchair landed on its side, which partially protected her from the falling debris. Terrel and Martha continued to dig in that same area, hoping that Sean might be there. Martha found a small hand under a board. She reached under, and the hand was warm but wet. She pulled her hand out, covered with blood. She knew that small hand had to be Sean's.

"Over here, Terrel!" Martha said. "It's Sean! I know it is. His hand is still warm, he's got to be alive."

Other homeowners in the area had called the police for help after hearing the explosion and help was on the way. Because there was so many phone calls about the explosion, the operator sent as many people as she could get. It had only been about seven or eight minutes, but to the O'Neills, it probably felt like seven or eight hours. The sirens were getting louder.

Terrel said, "Help is coming. Keep digging, we have to get him out. Stay with us, Sean, you have to live."

Two patrol cars and two fire trucks arrived—help had arrived!

"Over here!" Terrel called to the fire fighters. "Susan is right there, and I think that Sean is under here."

Three firefighters came running to help, and then it seemed like a whole army of them. "There's a small hand under here," Terrel said. Just the thought of a child being trapped turned the firefighters into Supermen. They will do whatever it takes. No statement reignites higher than to hear that a child is trapped. The firefighters and police pulled and pushed the debris to free the child.

Susan was the first to be freed from the debris and had already been carried to a safe area and was being worked on at the road. Sean was almost free. His hand had blood all over it from him wiping the blood off his face. Sean was in a bad way and had lost some blood from the beating that James gave him, compounded with the debris of the explosion that made it hard for him to stay conscious. Then Sean muttered, "Dad, Dad!" The firefighters knew that the children were probably not there by themselves. Sean's faint word of *dad* was all they needed to continue digging. One of the firefighters heard Sean and yelled to the other firefighters; the dad had to be under this debris somewhere. Sean heard a voice he recognized say that the dad was under there somewhere. "Find him!" Sean tried to listen; then he recognized that voice! That voice was Captain Whinnery. Hearing his voice gave Sean sense of comfort, comfort that his beaten body desperately needed. He knew help was here! As soon as Sean's feet were freed, he passed out.

The firefighters continued to dig through the rubble. Susan was being transported to the hospital, her wheelchair, even though she hated it, just saved her life and from serious injury. Sean was being loaded up into the ambulance, still unconscious yet somehow able to hear everything that was going on. The paramedic was covering Sean with a blanket to get him warm when something unusual caught her eye; it was Sean's crotch.

Sean's pants were not just wet from urine, but it looked like he was peeing blood. The paramedic quickly cut Sean's pants off because of the amount of blood on his pants. She figured there had to be a large wound that needed pressure. His pants were completely removed; no open wound. "Just blood-soaked pants." Just then, Sean started to pee thick blood-soaked urine. The paramedic told her partner, "He must have internal bleeding, we got to get him to the hospital now."

Sean was able to hear one of the firefighters say, "That house blew up like a bomb hit it, there is a twenty-foot crater in the backyard." The paramedic who was tending to Sean said that these two kids were lucky to be alive; they must've had a guardian angel looking out for them.

With those words, guardian angel, Sean started coming to. He was strapped to a board and his body was twitching from the tremendous amount of energy that he had expelled incinerating the man who had tried to kill his family.

"Mom? Dad? Where are my mom and dad?"

The paramedic had a voice like an angel. She said, "We will find them. My name is Melanie. I'm a paramedic with the fire department. What's your name?"

"Sean, Sean O'Neill."

"You're going to be okay?" she asked. "Who else was in your house when it blew up?"

Sean was still dazed and confused, and now was starting to get upset because he was tied down on a board and couldn't understand what was going on. His blood pressure was going up, his pulse is quickening. The paramedics saw that he was starting to panic.

"Calm down, Sean, you're safe," Melanie said. "Sean, you're with me in the ambulance. There was a terrible explosion at your house." Sean's blood pressure continued to climb. His pulse raced, and he started to expand heat. The paramedic knew something was wrong. Melanie said, "I'm going to give you a little something to help you relax." She put a little sedative in his IV drip, and he started to calm down and go back to sleep. "You feel the heat that was coming off of him?" she asked the driver of the ambulance.

The driver responded, "I didn't know where the heat was coming from."

Melanie stared at Sean. She thought to herself, *He's completely dry! His skin is cold and dry!* She had been on hundreds of calls, maybe even thousands, and seen lots of things over her five years of experience. Her mind was racing, but nothing like this was in any of her textbooks. She looked up at the driver and said, "Let's get him to the hospital. The doctors will have to figure this one out."

Terrel and Martha could only stand back and watch. As the ambulance pulled off, they both felt the presence that they were looking for in the yard was leaving. Somehow Sean was now recognizable as a Milky. Martha looked at Terrel; they both thought the same thing, "We can sense this human!"

With so many fire trucks and now police cars on the scene, Martha's car was pinned in; they couldn't go to the hospital and be with Sean. All they could do was watch and wait for some of the emergency vehicles to finish up. The rescue personnel knew they still had at least two more people to find. They were very sure that the mom and dad had been in the house, but nobody had any knowledge about Clinton. The firefighters were diligently looking for the other survivors; they had uncovered two kids and both of them were alive, so their hopes there still high.

Sean had told them that his mom and dad were at the house, so the search went on. The firefighters concentrated on the area where they found the kids.

Captain Whinnery got on his blow horn and said, "Everybody! Stop, turn all engines off, and listen."

Captain Whinnery called out, "Mr. and Mrs. O'Neill, this is Captain Whinnery of the fire department! If you can hear us, tap on something! If you can hear us, help us find you!"

Everybody was quiet and listening intently—nothing. Everybody went back to digging and sorting through the rubble for thirty more minutes and then stopped again. The police and firefighters continued to search, hoping that they were alive. The firemen continued to search the area between the front of the house and where they found the children. This went on for several cycles and no luck. Then the horn sounded again, and everybody stopped and listened.

A faint *tap, tap, tap, tap.*

"Over here!" One of the firefighters yelled. "The sound is coming from over here."

Everybody rushed to the area and dug faster. There was a wall section, and the sound was coming from underneath it, and the firefighters continued to break apart the wall section. One of them yelled, "I see hair!"

"Here, it's a man, he's alive! He's alive!" The firefighters presumed that the man was Mr. O'Neill. The firefighter called to Mr. O'Neill, "Hang in there, Mr. O'Neill, we will get you out."

As the firefighters continued to dig, there were still no signs of Mary. The firefighters found Mr. O'Neill buried next to a large rock in the front yard with a section that was like a roof over him. Jeffrey was in bad shape from the explosion, but that rock saved his life. Nearly all the crushing weight of the roof was being supported by the rock. The task of freeing Mr. O'Neill took the firefighters about another thirty minutes; the whole time, they were trying to ask him questions, but nothing Mr. O'Neill said made any sense.

Just then, another firefighter yelled, "Guys, over here." He had found the lower part of an arm! They looked at it and said, "That is not Mrs. O'Neill's arm, this is a man's."

Captain Whinnery came up to Jeffrey and asked, "Who else was in the house besides you and the two kids?"

Jeffrey was still muttering unrecognizable sentences.

Captain said, "We can't understand what you're saying, but if you can understand us just blink."

Jeffrey looked at him and blinked.

"Okay, one blink for yes and two blinks for no. Okay?"

Jeffrey blinked once. "Okay. Was your wife in the house?" Jeffrey blinked once. "Was there anyone else in the house besides you, your wife, and your two kids?" Jeffrey blinked once. "How many other people were in the house?" Jeffrey started blinking uncontrollably. "Take it easy," Captain Whinnery said. "Take it easy, and let me think of a better way for you." Jeffrey blinked once, reaching for Captain Whinnery's pen. Jeffery couldn't talk much, but he thought he could scribble something! Captain looked at it, trying to figure out what it said. "Does this say two strangers?" Jeffrey motioned to get the paper back and scribbled something else.

Captain Whinnery's eyes got big. "*Kill us?*" Jeffrey blinked once.

The paramedics said, "Captain, we need to get him to the hospital."

Captain nodded and called over a deputy. He showed the deputy the writing and said that somebody needed to stay with the O'Neill's at the hospital until they find out what's going on.

Another firefighter called for Captain Whinnery, "Sir, you might want to look at this."

There was a heavily scorched area on the floor that had the shape of a human body…but no body. Captain Whinnery was staring at the human shape, heavily scorched into the floor and then looked around. "What in the name of God happened here tonight?" Captain Whinnery looked up at the sky as if he were looking for heavenly guidance to explain what he was seeing.

The weather was now starting to take a toll on all the first responders. The cold, the snow, and now a human imprint scorched into the floor of what used to be the house. The snow continued to fall much heavier now. As he walked away shaking his head, he thought to himself, "This is going to be hard scene to sort through in the morning with all the snow." He blew the air horn again. Everybody was quiet and listening carefully, but nothing…not a sound.

"Keep looking," he said. "Keep digging!"

"Sir, over here." It was just the lower torso and legs of a man. "This guy must've been close to the source of the explosion."

The snow continued to fall, making the job harder. The firefighters were dirty, wet, and cold.

Even though the cold temperatures were starting to get to the first responders, nobody wanted to give up the search for Mrs. O'Neill or the rest of the mysterious man.

"Here, over here!" Two of the other men found the body of Mrs. O'Neill. It was heavily burnt on the back half. Most of the front half had clearly been facing away from the fire.

She must have tried to get out!

Captain Whinnery said, "Mr. O'Neill is going to lose his mind." He remembered that this was one of the families that was at the pool tragedy a few months ago. The captain was reliving the O'Neill's loss as if it were just yesterday; he lost his oldest daughter in an accident, and now tonight, his wife. "Rope off this entire area, and we'll come back in the morning when the snow slows down and the sun comes up."

Just then, another firefighter said, "I found the rest of that guy. The face was entirely burned off, and the chest cavity had caved in."

The firefighters had more questions than answers at this time. What caused such a massive explosion at this home, and who were those other two people. One was blown apart. What made the impression burned in the middle floor? Who were the people Mr. O'Neill said was in the house?

So many questions at this fire, and as of now...no answers.

Two deputies watched the house the rest of the night. Everyone else left waiting for daybreak. Daybreak came, and the snow had finally stopped, but not before dumping nearly twenty inches of heavy, packed snow. Captain Whinnery was standing in front of the station and staring at the snow.

"It may be spring before we get to see everything underneath all that snow," he said to himself. He walked back inside. Captain Whinnery picked up the phone to call the sheriff and find out what time the investigating team would meet them out at the O'Neill house to investigate the explosion.

Assistant Deputy Chief Brian Lampkin answered the phone. "Georgetown sheriff's office."

"This is Captain Whinnery. I'm trying to get a hold of the sheriff."

Chief Lampkin said, "We've been trying to get a hold of them since last night after that explosion. We found his truck out in the area, but he was nowhere to be found. At first we thought maybe he was hunting in the woods, but with an explosion as loud as it was, he would've made his way back either to that house or back here at the station."

"When can your team meet our fire investigators out at the scene?" Captain Whinnery said.

Chief Lampkin answered, "We will go down to the rental store and get as many heater blowers as we can and then we'll meet you about ten o'clock. Will that give you enough time to make sure there was not a gas leak in the area?"

Captain Whinnery responded, "My guys have already come back from the house, and there are no gas leaks detected in the area."

The fire investigators headed down to the O'Neill house, or at least the areas were the house was; Captain Whinnery headed to the hospital. He wanted to find out as much information as he could before he went to the house. Nothing added up yet, and now the sheriff was missing also.

The captain didn't want to point any fingers, but he knew that the sheriff had been hanging out with some shady people and wondered if he had something to do with the explosion. He told himself, *Too many questions.*

Captain Whinnery arrived at the hospital and was walking toward Mr. O'Neill's room. "Good morning, Captain," said Chief Lampkin.

"Good morning, Chief. I see you're here for answers too. Any word from Chief White yet?"

"No communications or sign of him. It's almost like he just disappeared. Last night at the house, we found pieces of an unidentified man and an area that appears to be the ignition point of the fire. We still don't know who the unidentified man is, but I'm hoping Mr. O'Neill can fill in some of the blanks."

The doctor came out of the room and started talking to Captain Whinnery and Chief Lampkin. The doctor said, "Mr. O'Neill's voice is a little hard to hear, but if you want to talk to him, I think that it will be okay. You guys can go see him, but first, I need to tell you the family was definitely drugged with ammonium nitrate. The father, mother, and the daughter had large amounts still in the blood system. The boy doesn't have any left in his system, but all of them did suffer from smoke inhalation."

"Thank you, Doctor," Captain Whinnery said. They went into the room. Jeffrey was lying in bed with bandages on both arms and on the right side of his face.

Chief Lampkin said, "Mr. O'Neill, we have so many questions and so little answers. Do you feel up to talking about what happened last night?"

There was so much anger in Jeffrey's face as he stared out the window; his head slowly turned and looked at the two uniformed men in his room. Jeffery said, "Really? You're going to stand there and ask me about last night? Really!"

Captain Whinnery stepped forward and calmly asked, "Jeffrey, do you mind if I sit next to you and talk for just a few minutes? We will leave whenever you want us to. We're just trying to come up with some answers. Can you help us…help you?"

Jeffrey said, "It was a beautiful night. We were sitting on the front porch watching the snow fall. It was beautiful. Then we came inside, and then we were in the living room watching TV."

"Who is we?" Chief Lampkin asked?

"Mary, Susan, and myself. Sean hadn't come home yet. He went over to the Mahoneys' house. We were watching TV, and we were all getting so sleepy." Jeffrey chuckled a little. "Susan fell so fast asleep, she almost fell out of her chair. Mary and I heard her book hit the floor. Mary got up to go get her to make sure she didn't fall out of her chair, and she collapsed on the floor. Seeing Susan slumped over in her chair was funny, but then when Mary fell, it wasn't funny anymore. I got up, and I was so dizzy. I felt like I was going to collapse also. I tried to get to the front door, thought maybe if I could open the door, you know…get some fresh air. I guess I hit the door, and then I guess I passed out on the floor just like Mary, and…and…and the next thing I remember was coughing, there was a fire."

"What was burning?" Captain Whinnery asked.

"I couldn't tell who he was."

"Don't you mean what was burning?"

"No, it looked like there was a man on the floor actually burning. I know what I saw. There are things that happen in life that you don't forget…like seeing a body on the floor engulfed in fire. I guess

Mary and I woke up about the same time and made our way outside. I tried to catch my breath and went back in to get Susan. When I got to Susan, I grabbed her and pulled her outside. I looked at the fire to see if I could put it out and that's when I saw Sean was on the floor also. I don't know when he got in the house, but he was lying on the floor near the guy that was burning. The fire was starting to spread pretty fast, and Sean wasn't moving. Then I went back in and pulled Sean…he was like a brick on the floor. I could barely move him. I never thought I was going to get them out! I pulled and pulled and the two of us made it outside, and then before I could turn around, the house exploded like a bomb. I swear there was another explosion, but maybe it was an echo. Part of the house hit me and knocked me to the ground. Next thing I remember, I tried to move. Whatever was on me was too heavy, I just couldn't move. I couldn't get up to go get my Mary. She was still on our front porch, and now she was burnt alive."

Just then, a priest knocked on the doorway and let himself into the room. Jeffrey was still looking down at his burnt arms and hands when he heard Chief Lampkin say, "Good morning, Father."

Jeffrey looked up with a furious look on his face. "Get out!" Jeffrey said in a very snarling voice. "What has my family ever done to you or your God! You stole my heart, you stole my love. I don't need your pity or your God's pity! What did I do to your God to make him steal the love of my life, kill my daughter, and cripple my other daughter? Oh, wait, Father, there's more…and put my only son in the hospital also! What did I do to you?"

Jeffrey had so much built-up anger and frustration in his life that the very presence of a religious man set them over the top. It was nothing personal to the priest, but it was very personal to Jeffrey.

The priest said, "God did not do this to you."

And before the priest could finish his sentence, Jeffrey grabbed the food tray and slung it across the room at him. "Get out of here!" He screamed. "Out!"

Chief Lampkin said, "Calm down, he is just here to talk to you."

Two nurses came running into the room. Jeffrey's pulse rate was rising; his heart was beating out of his chest. The heart monitor was going crazy and beeping alarms were going off.

Captain Whinnery was looking at the monitors. "He's crashing, he's crashing."

Two nurses came running with the crash cart and quickly tried to settle Jeffrey down. Then one nurse said, "You are all too much for him right now…way too much! Out! All of you, out!" The nurse grabbed a sedative and injected it into his IV. The other nurse said, "All of you out, everybody, out!"

The nurse worked to calm Jeffrey down and the other was like she had an invisible broom, sweeping everyone else out of the room and quickly closing the door.

Chief Lampkin and Captain Whinnery were talking in the hallway. "Well, Mr. O'Neill's story coincides with the family being gassed, but the rest of the story doesn't make sense," Chief Lampkin said.

"Sounds like somebody was trying to rob them. But why go through the trouble of gassing them? If you were just going to rob them," Captain Whinnery said. "I've met the O'Neills just a few months ago, they don't have very much as far as material things. It really sounds like someone was trying to kill the whole family, not rob them."

Chief Lampkin said, "I never thought I'd see this in our town, this is nuts! I've met the O'Neills before also, they're good people. I don't get that anyone would want to hurt this entire family. This just does not make sense. I think the boy may have some answers, maybe he saw something different. You remember what the doctor said that the father, mother, and daughter had gas in their system, but the boy did not, but all of them suffered from smoke inhalation? That means the boy may not have been in the house when the family was gassed."

"He may be the key," said Captain Whinnery. "Let's go talk to Sean. This seems to be the only thing that makes sense so far."

Chief Lampkin and Captain Whinnery entered the room that Susan and Sean were sharing. Susan was still asleep, but Sean was awake.

THE COMMON MAN

Captain Whinnery was smiling at Sean and said, "Good morning, do you remember me?" Captain Whinnery was looking around the room and then looking at these two children all bandaged up. He was thinking to himself that these two kids' lives are probably scarred for many years to come. This has been a year that nobody will be able to forget. Chief Lampkin and Captain Whinnery both put on a fake smile.

Sean gave a little smile and retuned the greeting, "Good morning, sir."

Captain Whinnery responded, "Do you mind if we come in for just a little bit and talk to you?"

Sean said, "Sure, but what do you mean that we will probably be scarred for life?"

"I don't recall saying that," Captain Whinnery said. "However, I was thinking that very thing."

Chief Lampkin said, "Help me figure out what happened last night. Sean, do you remember anything about last night?"

Sean had a very blank look on his face, and then his facial expression changed to very upset.

"It's okay," Captain Whinnery said. "Nobody's going to hurt you. You're safe here with me. Can you tell me about last night?"

"He tried to kill me! He tried to kill all of us!" Sean blurted out.

Captain Whinnery said, "Slow down, Sean, who?"

"The sheriff!" Sean said. "The sheriff."

Chief Lampkin said, "Slow down, start over, and relax! Your dad said that you were over at the Mahoneys' house. Try to start from there, what happened last night? Do you remember what happened?"

Sean was trying to slow his breathing down. "I went over to Zeke's house, and they were making a hockey ring. Then I came home, and it was really snowing, so I went to the back of my house so that I could make snow angels."

Sean stopped for a second, remembering his sister Luna, that she loved making snow angles.

Sean continued, "I had my eyes closed making a nice one when I heard the man say to me, 'I gotcha now.' I tried to get up, and he hit me in the head with something." He pointed to the large bandage on his head.

"Did you see who it was?" said Chief Lampkin.

Sean quickly said, "It was the sheriff! He carried me with my coat and said I can die in the house like all the rest of my family."

Chief Lampkin tried to get Sean to make sure what he was saying, "Are you sure it was…"

Sean interrupted, "It was him! Then he brought me inside and threw me on the floor. Mom and Dad were on the floor not moving. He called me a freak, and then he kicked me on the floor really hard. He was standing next to me, so I grabbed his leg, and it started to burn."

"What do you mean it started to burn?" Captain Whinnery said.

"He started to catch on fire and fell to the floor. It was like my hands were glued to him. His face was staring at me like I was a monster, and then he started screaming, and I couldn't move, and then the next thing I remember was my Dad was helping me out of the house. Then the whole house blew up."

Chief Lampkin said, "We found someone else at the house. Do you know who it was?"

"Somebody else carried Mr. Clinton into the house and threw him on the floor too."

"Was it, the sheriff?" Chief Lampkin asked?

"No, some other guy."

"You sure it was the sheriff at your house?" asked Chief Lampkin.

"Yes, he's the one who hit me in the head and then threw me on the floor," Sean said defiantly.

A nurse walked in the room. "Excuse me, Chief Lampkin. There's a call for you at the front desk." The chief followed her out of the room.

"This is Chief Lampkin."

A coroner at the morgue said, "You might want to come down here to the morgue and look at this guy. There's something really, well, different about this guy. Even though the body is burnt pretty badly, you can still see this."

Chief Lampkin and Captain Whinnery headed down to the morgue and went inside and were greeted with great enthusiasm.

The coroner could hardly wait to share what she had found. "I've seen a lot of strange markings, but not like this before." The coroner was talking really fast with excitement. "It says M5531 on the back of his ear. This looks more like an engraving than a tattoo. If having this engraving wasn't strange enough, this man is clearly well into his fifties, but his bone structure is that of a twenty-year-old man. That's not even the best part! All the organs in his chest are gone! Also, he has no fingerprints... I guess what I'm trying to tell you, Sheriff, is, I have no idea the age of this victim or his identity! This guy is a ghost!"

Chief Lampkin said, "This just keeps getting better. We know for sure the sheriff appears to be involved or may have been the burnt body on the floor, and now we have a non-aged, unidentified man who was at the house and blown apart."

Oden was waiting for Martha at Mark's house. He was very aware of everything that had taken place at the O'Neill home.

Martha, Terrel, and Robert arrived at the house to find Odin still there. Martha walked in the house was surprised that Oden was waiting for them.

Martha gave a quick acknowledgment to Oden. Martha said, "Oden, Sean is alive and at the hospital."

Oden replied, "I am aware of that, but that is not the reason for me being here. One of you must go to the morgue unnoticed and disintegrate the remains of Clinton. He deserves a chance to return to the heavens."

This was the first notice that Terrel had gotten about Clinton dying. "I didn't think it was possible to be killed as a human," Terrel said.

Oden said, "He was not killed by the hand of man or by the order of the Council or by another Milky guard. He was alive when the explosion hit him and severed his body in pieces. This happened because Clinton sacrificed his life to save his Jumper by gifting him in a dying gesture his powers so that the Jumper could save himself."

Terrel wanted to be the one to go to the morgue; Clinton had been his partner for several years.

Terrel made it to the morgue unnoticed. For such a small funeral home, the morgue had a lot of storage drawers for bodies. Terrel had to open up the morgue's refrigerated body drawers one by one. After three drawers with other people in them, he found Clinton.

The coroner had sewn him together the best that she could. Terrel was deeply moved by the sight of Clinton's lifeless body and saw what was left of his partner. Terrel stood there, looking at the parts of Clinton's body and how it was sewn together. His lip started to quiver, and his breathing started to shake. A tear started to come down his face. It surprised him! As he wiped it away, he had never experienced grief before. *What a strange feeling*, he thought to himself. He was experiencing his first emotion, a genuine human emotion because he developed a real friendship with Clinton and that they had gotten so close. His eyes were clouding over, and his lip couldn't stop twitching. The more he tried to stop his eyes from crying, the more tears poured out and ran down his face. His stomach started to ache, and his body started to shake. He was having real emotions and didn't know what to do with them. He continued wiping the tears away, but he just kept crying. There was an aching feeling in his abdomen. His entire body developed a slow tremble. He said only one word, "Clinton." Before he could even say anything else, he heard a sound in the hallway, bringing him back to the task at hand. He tried to tell Clinton that he was going to miss him, but somebody was coming. "Goodbye, my friend." Terrel had never spoken that word before, and he put his two hands on Clinton's body and disintegrated it into a small pile of ash in the refrigerator draw. "Goodbye, my friend."

CHAPTER 10

Eileen had finally worked up the nerve to speak to Tran about Paul. Unbeknownst to Eileen, after so many years of close contact with a human, she was developing human organs, and the first organ is always a heart, and that started her transformation into a human.

Eileen was ready for a change for Paul's welfare. She told Tran, "You know the Council will not stop trying to find Paul." Eileen continued, "I think it may be time for us to start introducing Paul to the real world in which he will be living. The last couple of times that we had to move Paul, we've made that move because of something that you instigated.

Tran said, "This boy is different. Zimbabwe has had me work with several humans over the decades, but this one special."

Eileen said, "I truly believe that he has absorbed some of our abilities from being close to us for so many years."

Tran responded, "Abilities? It's a lot more than that. Several years ago, I allowed him to sink his nails into my skin. With both hands drawing blood from me at the same time, he was able to receive a piece of my powers. The last time he drew blood from my leg, it took me a week to recover. Paul is going to be a human that will be talked about for years."

Eileen said, "Years? This is why he has the mood swings, you did this to him. He has a dark side of him that you have kindled for the last couple of years, and now you tell me. With his ability to draw energy from others, he is going to be difficult to steer."

Tran said, "I think Zimbabwe wants a new czar in the world. Why else would he have us keep Paul off the grid for so long? I can't wait to see what Zimbabwe is going to do with him after his HEART test. I can feel he is going to be the next Caesar! There hasn't been a leader like Caesar in over a thousand years, and I personally want a piece of this. I definitely want to be on his side!"

Eileen said, "We need to contact Malaywah. Paul needs humans to take care of him. He's getting too strong even for you to control. His HEART test isn't for another four years. That's four more years of him absorbing our abilities into his own." Eileen continued, "He already speaks four languages and can fight humans over twice his size with ease. At this pace, in four years, he will be unstoppable."

Tran said, "I realize that. Why do you think I want to be on his side?"

Eileen quickly cut Tran off, "His side! Really, let me tell you how I see it. You are trying to make him everything you're not, and Paul is a human. You are forcing him to be something he may not want to be. He is taking all the abuse of becoming the human that you're not because he idolizes you."

Tran said, "You are starting to talk like a human. I think I need to talk with Zimbabwe about having you removed. I think the way you are talking, you may be turning. In case you have forgotten, we are Milkies, and our job is to steer our candidates the way we're told to steer them."

Eileen responded, "Is that why we have to move one or two times a year? I'll answer for you. The reason we constantly have to move is because you keep making Paul do things that the other humans either find offensive or illegal."

Tran said, "Illegal? There is nothing illegal about training. Paul needs to train."

Eileen responded, "You're not training him. He's like your prized stallion, and you parade him around just so that somebody sees him and hopefully picks a fight with them."

Tran said, "He will be a force to reckon with when his time comes, and you can either be on his side or struggle on the other side. Czars are rulers, and Paul will be a powerful czar, and I will see to that."

Eileen walked away, muttering to herself, "You're going to get him killed before he even has a chance to be revealed to the world at his HEART test."

Tran said, "I guess you forgot I can still hear you."

Eileen shook her head and said, "He still has not recovered from the blood poisoning he received in Japan. He nearly died, and all you would do is pump up his ego. When he runs into another boy like that one in Japan, he will probably die, and you will be the one to blame. I assure you the Council will hear about that."

Tran and Eileen continued to squabble back and forth like a normal human couple when Paul walked into the room.

"I can hear you guys all the way back in my room," Paul said.

Eileen said, "Sorry, Paul, Tran and I were just discussing your training from this point forward."

"That is not what we were discussing," Tran quickly and abruptly cut off Eileen. "You are going to become the warrior that this world needs. I'm going to train you even harder, make you even stronger."

"You're going to kill him," Eileen blurted out.

"I'm doing just fine," Paul said. "Look how I did against those three boys in Japan."

"Exactly," Eileen said. "You almost died and spent the next year and a half recovering."

"That doesn't count," Paul said. "I still won!"

Tran said, "Eileen, you weren't there, you didn't see what happened. If you really want to know, I'll tell you."

Eileen said, "Sure, tell Paul how you almost killed him, go ahead, tell him."

Tran said, "Paul, that's not true. You and I had been practicing in the alley behind Yushiki's bar for almost a month."

"I remember," Paul said.

Tran answered, "What you don't remember is group of local boys that always had to come by when we were out there. The day of the fight, there were two extra boys that came by, and the reason you don't remember everything is because you got sick.

"The fight started because I wanted to see how much better you had gotten since the last time you fought. The last fight you are in was too easy. I wanted you to be in a battle that would last more than just a few minutes, so I figured since there were five of them, this would last a little while. As the boys were walking by, they did their normal insults at you except one thing. I turned my back and walked away and then sat down to watch. When I turned back around, the one boy came up behind you and kicked you in the back, and the fight was on. The first two boys were pretty big, maybe four or five years older, and the three of you worked each other over pretty good. That's when things went bad. The boy who kicked you in the back tried to stab you. You kicked the knife out of his hand, picked it up, and slashed them across the chest. When you came in contact with his blood, instead of getting stronger, you started to shake. And they all started beating on you. I thought that once you came in contact with the other boy's blood that he would make you stronger again the way that I have seen you do so many other times in the past. But this was different. After I killed the one boy and the rest of them ran away, you just lay there, shaking and bleeding. I had no way of knowing that the blood from that sick boy would make you so sick. I soaked my hand in the blood of the boy and then put it on your wound thinking that you would start getting strong again, but I think that the boy had a virus. You stopped shaking and went unconscious. I had no way of knowing that that boy had a virus."

Paul said, "Why have you not told me this before? How come you two had to start arguing before I knew this? This happened almost a year and a half to two years ago, and you're just telling me now why I've been so sick for so long. Is everything you're saying to me a lie? Who am I?" And with that, Paul ran out of the house.

This was not the first time that Paul ran away from Tran, but this would be the first time that he really tried to run away. Paul was walking through the alleys just looking for a quiet place to sit and think. Straight up ahead was a large body of water with several piers sticking out into the water. He picked the one that looked the most deserted and walked out to the end and sat down. There was a boat tied to the pier on both sides.

As the saying goes, bad luck always has company, and Paul ended up not alone at the end of that pier.

Two ladies were sorting through the day's catch from the fishing trip and yelled over to Paul that this was a private pier, yelling, "You have to go!" Paul put his hand up and signaled to them, sorry, got up, and turned around and walked off their pier.

Paul thought to himself, *I can't even run away without getting in trouble.* Just about that time, he looked up—it was Eileen.

Eileen called out to Paul, "I came down here to look for you because if it was me trying to get away, this is where I would've gone to. Being an orphan, I'm sure life has been tough on you, but I tried my best to take care of you. I think it may be time for you to be around other people. Come on. Let's get out of the cold."

Over on the northern border of Pennsylvania, Robert has just arrived at the hospital to do a welfare check and was walking into the O'Neill's hospital room. It was one of the largest patient rooms at the hospital, and all three of the O'Neills were in it. Robert looked around—Jeffrey, Susan, and Sean. Sean! The image of Sean brought back an immediate flashback of his last encounter with the boy. Sean had touched him and had been able to read what he was thinking. Robert knew he had to be careful. He grabbed a chair and moved it over in front of Sean.

"Sean, I know you have talked to a lot of people about what happened that night your house blew up, but can you tell me again as much as you can about what happened that night. Start with when you came home from the Mahoney house."

Sean said, "I already told you. I was making a snow angel, and then the sheriff hit me in the head. I woke up, and I hurt all over, but especially my head, and then the sheriff picked me up by my coat and told me I could die in the house with the rest of my family. I tried to get away, but he was too big and then he beat on me again. He brought me in the house. He said I was the one to blame for all this…"

Robert said, "Relax, Sean, I just want to see if you remembered anything else."

"I saw Dad and Mom and Mr. Clinton on the floor. Mr. Clinton was beaten up really bad and not moving. I thought he was dead. I started to get mad. I started to get really mad because he told me that my mom and dad were dead, and it was my fault. He called me a freak and kicked me on the floor really hard. I saw Mr. Clinton grab my leg. I thought he was dead. Then the sheriff started to kick me again. I was just trying to block his kick, and I grabbed his leg, and I couldn't let go. His leg started burning."

"It started to burn?" Robert asked. "What was burning?"

"I'm not lying!" Sean defiantly said. "It was like the fire was coming out of my hands, and I couldn't let go of his pants. He was screaming, but I couldn't let go. I was so mad because I thought my mom and dad were both dead, and then I heard was my dad coughing. So I yelled, 'Dad, Mom, the house is on fire!' I couldn't move. Finally, my dad grabbed me and dragged me outside. Dad had just put me down by Susan when the house blew up." Sean was crying. "My mom's dead, and it's my fault."

Robert tried to comfort Sean and said, "It's not your fault."

Sean said, "Yes, it is. The sheriff said it was my fault."

"No, Sean, the sheriff was wrong. He was to blame of your Mom's death, not you."

Sean's eyes were screaming, "Why!" And then Sean said, "Why did my hands put the sheriff on fire? Maybe I am a freak."

"No, Sean, you're very special, and I'm going to help you." Robert felt bad for the human boy and made the mistake of getting down on one knee in front of Sean to try and connect with him. Sean reached up and hugged Robert around the neck.

Touching Robert so close to his brain was like a giant charge of electricity to Sean. He saw all the way back to his earliest moments of his existence, when Paul was holding onto Sean's soul and looking through him, through his eyes. He saw inside the Mount Soul. There were names written on the inside of the wall. Sean started to read them out loud: Caesar, Alexander the Great, Kublai Khan. Robert pried Sean off his neck and stood up, dizzy and disoriented. Robert had a very confused look on his face.

"What did you just say?" Robert asked.

"These names are written on the inside of a wall…it was beautiful." Robert knew he had to get away.

Sean said, "Who is Paul?"

Robert was starting to panic. "I…I…I gotta go, Sean. I'm sorry, and I have to go right now!"

Jeffrey was still heavily sedated but started to get excited and said, "What are you talking about, Sean? And, Robert, where are you going? Caesar, Alexander the Great? What are you two talking about?"

Robert was a stuttering uncontrollably. All he could say was, "I'm not, I'm not…sure, well…um." Sean squeezed Robert's neck so hard that he was losing his ability to speak. Robert finally said, "I need to go outside. I need some fresh air. I'll be back, Mr. O'Neill. I'll be back."

Chief Lampkin and Martha entered the hospital at the same time, greeting each other while having small talk as they went down the hall when they saw Robert run out of the room, heading for the lobby door at a very fast pace. They went over to the room and went in and saw Sean was hugging Jeffrey. Sean's face was like stone, and Martha said, "Is everything okay?"

Jeffrey nodded, and the two of them left to try to catch up with Robert. Chief Lampkin yelled to Robert outside, "Robert, we need to talk."

Robert yelled back, "I'll get with you later, Chief. I have to go to the office right now." He waved goodbye as he drove away. He just wanted to get away from Sean, as far away as possible. He decided the safest place for him to be at was at Mark's house and to wait for Martha and Terrel to show up.

Two days passed, and Martha and Terrel still had not heard from Robert, and he did not show up at school. Martha called Terrel, "We need to find Robert. He is not at his house, and he hasn't shown up at school yet."

Robert was so shaken up from such a traumatic encounter that he did not turn his abilities back on yet, and therefore, other Milkies could not find him. All Robert wanted to do was get into a safe place to try to figure out what just happened, to try to start talking normal again, without a stutter, and to recover.

Terrel said, "If we don't find him by tonight, we will meet up at Mark's house and ask the Council for help. They will be there tomorrow anyways."

Martha and Terrel arrived at Mark's house and saw Robert's car there. Robert had not left Mark's house since he'd arrived two days ago. Robert opened the door and said, "I sure didn't think it would take you two days to find me. Get in here, we have to talk."

Just then, the house shook, and clouds were coming to the floor. It was Oden and Almighty Malaywah. Malaywah tapped his staff on the floor and said, "Everyone, have a seat."

Robert stood up and just started to blurt out everything on his mind.

His face still had a scared look to it, but that didn't slow him down. "I've never encountered a human with powers as strong as his. The boy incinerated the sheriff, James White. Clinton is dead, and he saw inside the Mount Soul chamber."

Oden said, "Slow down."

Robert said, "James was trying to kill the O'Neill family, and Sean grabbed him by the leg and incinerated him. He must've absorbed Clinton's powers while they were lying on the floor. While I was talking to Sean, I got too close to him, and he reached out and hugged me around the neck. It was like a strong electrical charge. He looked through me to see all the way back when he was holding on to Mount Soul. He was able to see into the Mount Soul chamber."

Oden said, "That's not possible."

Robert said, "He read off some of the names on the inside of the chamber: Caesar, Alexander the Great, Kublai Khan."

Malaywah stood up and the room went silent. He looked at his staff and then started to walk around in a circle. You could have heard a church mouse walk across the floor. Oden sat there patiently, waiting for some sort of response.

Malaywah then turned around and said, "For thousands of years, the Council has protected Jumpers. They are an essential part of the human species. It takes a special human to not just be a Jumper, but to identify himself as a Jumper, to have the ability and the desire to know that there is more for that person. However, this Jumper, this Sean, is different. This one is dangerous. He is about to turn thirteen years old, and he already possesses the ability of a full-grown Jumper. It is not unprecedented for a Jumper to be able to drain a Milky of his powers, but what is unprecedented is that he was able to use our weapon, the ability to disintegrate. If we cannot get him under control, I will have to handle this myself. A human cannot absorb our powers. Clinton must have known that his termination was imminent and therefore sacrificed himself and his powers to save his human. It was an honorable gesture, but the Council decides what abilities or gifts a human gets."

Oden was shocked. To his knowledge, Malaywah had only used his supreme power once before, when he had disguised himself as a desirable woman for Attila so that when Attila and his new bride were alone on their wedding night, he disemboweled him. Not even the mighty Attila could defeat the power of Malaywah.

Malaywah thought carefully for a few moments and finally said, "I will send you a new set of Milkies. You need to keep them cloaked, out of sight from the rest of the humans in the area. After all this… difficulty, the O'Neill's will surely want to move, and you are to have the new Milkies settle in as their new neighbors wherever they relocate." Malaywah stood up and looked at Oden, and without saying a word, Oden stood up, and Malaywah tapped his staff on the floor. The two of them disappeared into the floor.

After a couple of days, Martha and Robert returned to the hospital, making sure that their powers were as off as they could. They were standing outside with flowers. Martha was getting her game face on, how to find out as to where they were going to live when they get out of the hospital next week. She knew that flowers would bring a smile to Susan's face and make Jeffrey more relaxed.

Martha and Robert walked into the room, and Susan's face lit up. "Flowers," she exclaimed.

As Martha brought the flowers to Susan, Jeffrey smiled and said, "This is a nice surprise."

Robert said, "We've always told you that you're not in this town alone. We try to be there for all our kids."

Martha said, "I talked to the nurse, and she said that you all would be leaving probably next week."

Jeffrey said, "I have a pretty good job here, but I don't know if I can put my life back together. I don't think anyone could say they've had a worse year than we have."

While Jeffrey was talking, Martha was trying to read Jeffrey's mind and see where he was thinking of going. While she was doing that, Sean looked at her puzzled.

"Miss Ruby," Sean said, "why don't you just ask?"

Martha glanced at Sean with a surprised look and said, "You must be reading my mind. I was just telling myself that I hope you all stay around."

Jeffrey said, "Don't let him scare you. He's been getting pretty good at reading people's minds lately. It's like he can look right at you, and you can ask him a question in your mind, and he can answer you. It's almost like the explosion woke up an unused part of his brain. It's a little scary!"

Martha quickly checked her powers, thinking that Sean would stay out of her head. "I hope you will be planning to stay in the area. This is a good town, and I'm sure there are a lot of people who are going to be willing to help you put your lives back together," Martha said.

Jeffrey gave a little scowl and said, "This last year has been like poison. I don't know if there's anything left to put back together. My dad wants me to come back home. He said there's plenty of work in the area, and we will have a place to stay."

Robert said, "Where did you grow up?"

Jeffrey said, "Up on Schaghticoke Hill. It's real peaceful there, and the air tastes so clean. At this time of the year, we used to go down to the dam and play hockey. The kids need some fun, and I'm thinking pretty hard about my dad's offer. Besides, Schaghticoke Hill is not too far away, and the kids are almost old enough to come and see their friends if they want on their own. It's about an hour away, and there is plenty of work. But do I want to live with my dad and start all over again?"

Martha glanced at Jeffery and Susan; both still had a lot of bandages and needed a lot more time to heal. Sean's body had no bandages and had nearly healed. Sean definitely has Milky powers.

Sean could feel the energy from Robert and Martha. He knew something was different about them—a friendly warmth and a sense of calm, a feeling of almost like being a battery and being left on a slow charge. Martha sensed that Sean's senses were starting to heighten with two Milkies so close. Sean walked over and stood between Robert and Martha and looked at Jeffrey.

"Dad," Sean announced. "Things are going to get better. I'm going to become so powerful that nobody messes with us again. I've seen what I'm supposed to do in my dreams. I'm going to be just like Caesar. President O'Neill...nobody will mess with our family again."

"Stop that, Sean!" Jeffery said. "I'm sorry, Robert, ever since our house blew up, Sean seems to think that you can change up your stars. The boy doesn't listen. I've told him that the harder you work, the more the world will fight against you. This year should have told him that for sure, I worked sixty plus hours every week, all years, and God just took my life, chopped it up, rolled it into a ball, and then threw it away."

Martha said, "God didn't create this tragedy. Two men that did."

"Don't get me started," Jeffrey said, "and if I catch the one that got away..."

Robert interrupted Jeffrey and said, "Don't say it. His justice will come. It may not be today, but it will come."

"Nobody is even looking for him," Jeffrey said.

Martha said, "Chief Lampkin and the rest of the deputies will find that guy that got away."

Robert was looking around the room and saw Susan just lying in bed, not saying a word. Robert tried to change the subject and said, "Susan, what do you think of Schaghticoke Hill?"

No answer—just a quiet look.

Robert tried again to get Susan to join in the conversation, so he asked, "Has it been a long time since you were there? Your dad said you won't want to leave once you go see Pine Tree World."

Still no answer; Susan just turned her head and looked the other way.

Martha was still thinking about Schaghticoke Hill. It was an area she was not familiar with. She asked herself several questions: *How many people can we get into position before the O'Neill's relocate? Can we get somebody close enough to where Jeffrey's father lives to watch Sean? And how can I...*

Sean interrupts her thinking, "Miss Ruby, why do I need somebody to watch me?"

It had slipped her mind just for a moment that Sean could listen to her thoughts. She quickly interjected a question back at Sean. "Sean, how is it that you look like you're healing so fast?" Martha was really quick-thinking, trying to play off Sean's question with a question to him or at least humor.

Sean said, "Even my bruises are disappearing faster than I have ever seen. The doctor said I had two broken ribs."

Sean pounded on his chest like Tarzan.

"Doesn't hurt anymore. It's crazy, even my ribs healed fast."

Martha responded, "What! Must be nice to be a young man and heals so fast." She quickly tried to change the subject and directed her attention to Jeffrey. "I was just thinking about where your dad grew up and that how much we will miss your kids here. As a teacher, I get very attached to my kids," she said to Jeffrey.

Jeffrey said, "If it makes you feel any better, I have no desire to start my whole life over again. I don't know who is more scared, me or the kids." Jeffrey was staring at Susan; he could see the sparkle in her eye. She had the same sparkle that Mary had. A welling of emotions came over him. He missed his Mary something terrible. Mary was his rock, and now she was gone. All this was going through his mind as the tears started to flow. He felt like he was losing control, and without his Mary, he really didn't care. What started out as just a little tear were now the tears of a lonely and scared man.

Jeffrey said, "What did I do? What have I done that was so bad that everything had to be taken away from me?"

At times like this, Martha felt human and just wanted to scream out that none of this was about them. Sean was the one who was identified as a Jumper, not them. But the words and emotions couldn't come out.

Sean felt a chill down his back, the chill of fear. Sean started to look around with a terrified look. Jeffrey looked over at Sean and Susan and was lost in his own world. Martha and Robert both felt the cold go down their spines. Fear, they not only felt it, but they tasted it. Martha and Robert both looked at Sean. Sean walked to the window and looked out. "There's someone out there," Sean said. "I can see his eyes, and I feel him. I don't know where he is. His eyes are staring at me. One of the eyes is black as coal. The other one is as blue as the ocean."

"Who's out there?" Jeffrey said.

Robert looked out the window, "Sean, I don't see anybody."

Martha telepathically spoke to Robert, "That kind of fear is real, but also knowing that the cold of fear can make humans do strange things, I'll try to explain to Sean that there is nothing out there."

Sean turned around and snapped at Martha, "Why do you keep talking like I'm crazy? I can hear you."

Jeffrey said, "Sean, get away from that window. Nobody said anything like that to you."

Martha, sensing Jeffrey was getting upset and sensing the aggravation in his voice, changed the subject, "We want you to stay in the Georgetown area. I'm sure the entire staff at the school would pitch in to help you rebuild your life in any way we could. If you do decide to leave and you need help, you can call on us at the school, and we will be there for you."

The cold chill that was still reigniting down Sean's spine was Malaywah looking through a porthole into the hospital window. Malaywah could feel Sean's weakness (paranoia!). This was not just a thirteen-year-old boy's fear, but this was an internal fear, the kind of fear that you have deep down inside. Malaywah wanted to know Sean's vulnerability in case in the future he needed to exploit it.

Some people have a fear of spiders or water or even the dark, but this was Sean's Achilles' heel. That's something that everyone is born with that most people try to hide as they are growing up. Malaywah knew how to play with the vulnerabilities in humans. As the expression goes, he can play them like a fiddle.

Sean had a weakness. The cold chill that Sean felt was not the fear of another man, but the fear of being alone.

Sean lost his mom, and he worries about losing his dad.

Malaywah continued watching and observing Martha and Robert's every word. His presence was unbeknownst to everyone;

however, Sean sensed Malaywah's presence. Sean's heightened senses were a permanent gift from Clinton before he died. Malaywah watched Martha and Robert leave. Sean was talking to Jeffrey. Then Sean became quiet, turned around, and walked back over to the window again. Malaywah wanted to see for himself, whether or not Sean in fact possesses all of Clinton's abilities.

Sean could feel Malaywah's eyes; the cold chill came back down his spine, except this time, his hands started to get warm. Sean was scared—scared of the monster that he didn't know and terrified that the monster was going to hurt his dad again. Sean raised up his hands and, with anger at the window, said, "Leave my dad alone!" His hands started to glow as they were pressed on the glass of the window. He was fixed on the very thought of being alone and that completely terrified him.

"Sean!" Jeffrey said. "What are you doing? Your hands...look at your hands!"

In Sean's eyes, his hands looked normal. They just looked like two hands touching the glass.

"They're glowing!" Jeffrey said. "You don't see that?"

The caulking around the glass started to melt as the glass heated up, and then the glass fell out. Jeffrey yelled, "Sean!"

All the commotion in the room made Martha and Robert both step back into the room just in time to witness everything.

Susan was staring at Sean's hands, thinking that he was some sort of freak. Up until now, Susan just didn't like him because he was always the star, the apple in everyone's eye. Until Sean came along, she had been the star to everyone. Looking at his hands, her thoughts changed from sibling rivalry to fear. "Why are your hands glowing?" Susan asked.

Sean took two steps toward Jeffrey and Susan.

Susan said, "Stop! Don't come any closer." Susan was shaking and reaching out for Jeffrey.

Sean looked back at his hands, and they looked normal to him.

Martha was stunned—seeing is believing! There was no doubt that Sean possessed Clinton's abilities.

Jeffrey said, "What's going on with you? You can hear people's thoughts, and now your hands glow when you get mad." Jeffrey wanted to say something to the doctors about Sean but decided instead to try and figure it out on his own.

CHAPTER 11

Eileen tried to come up with every scenario to get rid of Tran but couldn't come up with a one that wouldn't affect Paul. He was thirteen years old and therefore still emotionally vulnerable going through puberty. She wanted out of this mess that she and Tran had created. "That's it!" she said to herself. "I'm going to do it. I'm going to contact Malaywah!"

A massive bolt of lightning hit the ground, and when Malaywah appeared. Eileen was ready. This was the moment that she had been waiting for for several years, and for several years, it had been a moment of guttural anguish, that feeling of whether or not she's doing it like the Council would have liked her to have done it. She knew that the day would come when turning Paul over to the Council would finally happen. But now she had developed real human emotions and caring for Paul, and to her, it was like raising a baby deer and then, after completely bonding with it, having to let him go. As Eileen was talking about the past ten plus years, Malaywah's eyes looked cold, and his staff was sparking like a Tesla oscillator.

Just then, Tran walked up and acknowledged Malaywah. Tran said, "We were just developing Paul the way Zimbabwe had instructed us to."

That was the proverbial last straw! Malaywah had enough, and without saying a word, with the same force as lightning, he projected his staff and struck Tran in the chest. He hit him so hard, it was like he was a paper bag that was full of flour and was just struck with a baseball bat!

Eileen's mouth dropped and her eyes were bulging wide open with anticipation that she was next, that she was no different than

Tran. She dropped to the ground, but it didn't happen. She stayed down on her knees and waited for her punishment, hoping not to be vaporized like Tran.

Malaywah said, "I will deal with Zimbabwe. Bring Paul to the orphanage here in Montreal run by Sister Joan, and so that nobody looks up his history, make the paperwork reflect that his name is now Paul Washington. He needs to be wanted and needed in order for him to have a chance in society. He is so far behind socially after having been under Tran's care, as well as so many physical differences with the birthmarks and the massive scars. He still may have a chance to be a successful Jumper. Unless you're holding back information from me, this is what has to be done."

Eileen said, "That's just about everything, and I'll make it happen."

In saying that, there was another massive bolt of lightning, and Malaywah was gone.

Before he left, Eileen explained to Malaywah why they had moved around so often, and that Tran had interacted with so many of the locals in so many countries that they were constantly moving. Tran would leave a trail of pain and misery to the locals, and she would have to go back to the locals and make things right. Most of the time they would ask them to leave and don't come back. Tran was much more powerful, and she dared not to cross him, but there was a lot more truth that did not come out. Like the fact that Paul not only had special abilities, but that he had been using them for quite some time and that he absorbed a tremendous amount of power in using his abilities with Tran. But the most important information that she held back was that Paul had an enormous weakness that could be exploited if anybody knew about it.

Paul knew this day would be coming because he was told that he was an orphan and that someday he may have to go to an orphanage to find a new family, and today was the day. The two of them drove away; Eileen tried to explain that Tran was gone in such a way that a thirteen-year-old boy would not feel guilty. Tran was Paul's mountain to climb, and now he felt like he was going to be dropped off in to middle of the ocean, no place to climb and no one to look up to. Paul looked up and saw the sign for Montréal's municipal orphanage.

Inside, Eileen was met by a Catholic nun, whose name was Sister Joan. Even though she was not a Milky, the Milkies all treated like she was one of them. When it comes to the sisterhood, Sister Joan was like the pope. Nobody messes with Sister Joan. It was either her way, or it was her way! She had the highest percentage of successful adoptions in Canada's history. Eileen knew that this was his best chance of having a good life.

Paul was introduced to Sister Joan. Paul had never met a real holy figure before and was humbled by her presence.

The way everybody walked and talked around her, she had the complete respect of everyone around her. This was a kind of power that Paul had never witnessed before—the power of respect instead of the power of force.

Sister Joan signaled to another sister, "Show Paul where he will be staying and then show him around the campus."

Paul saw a sign to sign up for a trip to Niagara Falls and asked if he would be able to go on that trip. The sister showing him around said, "If you are settled in, I don't see why not. Everybody loves a trip to Niagara Falls."

Eileen left the orphanage feeling like a human mother that just lost a child.

She had been with Paul so long that she had real human emotions of loss and separation. Now she would just wait on the Council to give her the next orders.

Martha, upon hearing that Sean would be leaving the hospital and heading to Schaghticoke Hill, contacted Oden. Oden contacted two Milkies in the Schaghticoke Hill area and had them start collecting information about where Sean would be living, going to school, and anyplace that he might go in the area. Both of the Milkies responded that they would start at the two restaurants in the area: Sammy's, and the favorite place in the area, the Schag A Val.

At the hospital in Georgetown, all three of the O'Neills were being discharged at the same time. Jeffrey's father was there to bring everyone back to his house on Schaghticoke hill.

The name of Jeffrey's father was Carl, but everybody called him Grampy.

"Grampy!" Susan exclaimed.

Grampy smiled, "Let's get you guys home. Maybe your dad will let us stop at the Schag A Val to grab some lunch. That is, if you guys are not already full of hospital food. The Schag A Val is the best little truck stop on the way home, it's worth the wait."

Sean said, "Count me in. Their vanilla shakes are what I love the best."

It was a short drive. Once the sign for the Schag A Val was in sight, everybody was smiling and ready for a good lunch. They all sat down, and while they were waiting for their food, Sean got up and walked over to a postcard display. Postcards from several places caught his attention.

Sean called to Grampy, "Grampy, where is Ruby Falls?

Grampy said, "It's in Tennessee."

Sean answered, "Can we go there?"

Jeffery cut in, "That's a long way from here."

Sean continued looking and found a card from Niagara Falls. "What about Niagara Falls?"

Susan said, "We have never been there. Dad said it's a long way away also."

Grampy said, "From here, it's not too far. I will make a deal with you guys. In a couple of weeks, once we have your school schedule adjusted, I'll take you all to go see Niagara Falls. If we can fit it into your new school schedule, and if your dad says it's okay."

Jeffrey smiled and said, "It's awfully cold this time a year to go see Niagara Falls, don't you think?" Jeffrey really didn't want to go anywhere or look that far ahead.

Grampy said, "A little cold, a little snow, maybe that is what this family needs. Besides, the mist from the falls makes everything all around there look like giant ice sculptures. I'm sure that Susan and Sean will enjoy it. You need this also." He looked at Jeffrey.

Sean said, "Do you think there will be enough snow for us to have a big snowball battle?" Grampy said, "At this time of year, there should be plenty, but for now, let's eat our lunch."

The news that Sean was at the Schag A Val didn't take long to be relayed to Oden. At the same time, Oden received an update about Paul Washington that he was settling in well at the orphanage and was interested about the field trip to Niagara Falls.

Oden called Martha. "I just received two messages from the Council. First one said that there stands a high chance that Paul Washington will be at Niagara Falls in a couple of weeks. The second message that just came in was about Sean and the entire O'Neill family planning to travel to Niagara Falls in a couple of weeks. There is a good likelihood that the two of them will be in a very close to the proximity to each other. This could start a ripple effect that would be hard to slow down. I know that you have grown attached to Sean and are sidelined now that Sean has been moved. You are all still in play in this area, and I am just keeping you informed."

Martha said, "Can you tell me something about Paul? Has he started to develop an ability? If so, what is it, and what could potentially happen if they were to meet?"

Oden said, "There is no report that Paul has started developing abilities yet, and I can't even imagine what could happen if they meet. They cannot be allowed to meet until they both have completed their HEART test. I don't think anyone wants that to happen."

Robert was with Martha and asked, "What does that mean?"

Oden said, "Sean and Paul are traveling with a high likelihood that their paths could cross. The Council has a signal that covers, or should I say, covers the what-if scenario. It is rarely invoked. It's call signal 99. Let's hope that this is not the case."

Oden continued, "It's very rare for one soul to live after contact. Both Jumpers survived the sorting table and at least one has already been gifted Milky powers. The council is thinking that when and only when they do connect, they may be able to remember that humans have no choice in life. That their lives are preselected, and there may be a major revolt. This is all speculation, but any way you say it, the outcome will not go unnoticed."

"What could that really mean?" Martha asked.

Oden hesitated, "This could easily turn into a signal 99. No Milkies and no established backup for either Jumper are in place.

There will be three different teams all converging on Niagara Falls with the potential plan of invoking signal 99."

Martha took a deep breath and thought to herself, *This sounds bad for Sean.*

Martha said, "Signal 99! I have never heard of such a thing."

Oden said, "This would only be the third time that I know of that a signal 99 was invoked. You can expect at least ninety-nine dead, including one or both Jumpers. No human or Milky will be spared. Everybody has been warned, and the plans are put in place for signal 99. For everybody's sake, I hope it's not invoked."

Oden continued, "The goal is simple. Keep the Jumpers apart, and the threat will be gone, therefore, no signal 99. We have to get them through their HEART test. Once they both have gone through the debriefing, they will understand how things work and how to use their powers. If that is not simple enough, that's when the signal 99 will come into play."

Martha was devastated. She had grown attached to Sean, and to think that he could be taken out! Martha said, "Have the other Milky Guards been briefed on the possibilities of a signal 99?"

Oden said, "Felicia's briefing the three teams as we speak. She is telling them the same thing I am telling you. 'Keep Jumper Sean away from Jumper Paul at Niagara Falls.' All three teams that are converging on Niagara Falls know that a signal 99 means that a body count will be extremely high, and no one is exempted, *no one*! Mortal or immortal."

Robert said, "I wish I could find a way to make Sean come back to Georgetown."

Paul had been at the orphanage for just a short time and was not fitting in very well. The other kids thought that he had some sort of leprosy with the scars all over his body from his tough years growing up with Tran and the heavy scars on his hands and those webbed feet. The boys who were not tormenting him about those scars were making fun of the hairy giant claw mark on his back. Tran did one good thing for Paul. He gave Paul thick skin to let *most* things roll off his back. He hadn't lost his temper yet but had found a nice quiet place that he could hide nearly every day. Self-meditation was one of the gifts that Tran taught him, to come down and unwind. Yoga and cotta are disciplines that Tran focused hard on teaching.

Sister Joan had posted a sign in the lunchroom talking about the trip next weekend to Niagara Falls. This posting was different from the last one. This one had a place where you could write your name and sign up.

Sister Joan said to Paul that if he continued doing his chores and helping the younger boys, then he could go, even though he had only been there a short time. Sister Joan enforced the rules, and her rules were simple. No fighting, do your chores—those are the two that get most kids in trouble.

Paul was so excited that he was going to go on his first vacation. Paul said, "I've been all over the world, but I've never been to Niagara Falls."

Sister Joan responded, "Well, let's add this place to your list."

Sister Joan signed Paul on this trip with all the rest of the kids. The weather report stated a good chance for snow around the east end of the Great Lakes, which means Niagara Falls. When she said yes and finished writing Paul's name, Sister Joan had this strange feeling come across her. She pictured herself as if she was a fly in a small room with a bunch of lizards, or a mouse dropped into a room full of sleeping cats. She couldn't shake the feeling! All her senses were screaming, *Mayday! Mayday!*

Malaywah ordered a meeting of the Council to go over the plans for the three groups to disrupt Sean and Paul from meeting. Felicia and Oden are in charge of two of the groups because of their connection with the candidates. Both Felicia and Oden were invested in the preservation of their candidate. The other group would be run by Zimbabwe.

Zimbabwe was not at the meeting, so this was a tremendous shock to both Felicia and Oden. This was the perfect opportunity for Malaywah to test Zimbabwe's loyalty after hearing the information from Eileen and Tran. Zimbabwe had no concerns for anybody's life. As soon as Oden and Felicia heard that Zimbabwe was going to run the other group, they knew that no one would be safe. Oden and

Felicia each thought that they would be able to protect their candidate and try to deflect the other candidate away from each other.

Simple.

They would keep changing their directions for the few days that they are there, and they will both go back safely away and no signal 99.

This is why Malaywah sent a third group. Humans are not simple! With over a week for Zimbabwe to make the weather pattern change, hopefully one of the candidates would be persuaded not to go.

Sean had been watching the weather, and the more snow, the better for a great trip.

Jeffrey was starting to get a little nervous about the weather and said, "The weatherman is saying that there looks like a big snowstorm, could be fifteen to twenty-four inches."

Susan and Sean's answers were excitement. Sean was starting to feel the pressure from Jeffrey about staying out of his head, but to Sean, this was a new toy to play with. Sean was trying to use his new ability and relax his dad about the weather, but it was not working.

I need to keep testing myself, Sean told himself. Sean liked this new, strange feeling of being able to get into other people's minds.

Sean sent Jeffrey a telepathic message, *Sounds like there will be excellent snow sledding*.

Jeffrey thought to himself. *Building snowman and sleigh riding, this may turn into a great vacation*. But at the same time he thought about the drive out and back.

Sean had been working on his dad for days about the trip; however, his powers were not working the way he wanted them to. The reason that Sean's mind games weren't working was because Oden was in the background, reversing the thoughts that Sean was putting into Jeffrey's head. "Don't go! The weather is going to be too bad. The weatherman is always wrong."

Before Jeffrey could even digest the thoughts that Oden was putting in his head Sean broke in, "Don't be thinking like that, Dad. We will all have a great time."

Oden hadn't realized just how strong Sean's power was getting and decided to leave. Oden told himself there's other ways to get through to Jeffrey when Sean was not around.

Susan was regressing more and more away from Sean. She has been noticing the changes in her brother. How he can read minds was just a quirky thing to her, but after seeing his hands light up in the hospital room and knowing that their house burnt down made her scared of Sean.

The kind of scared that you feel deep down to your toes.

There was little anyone can do to change your mind.

Susan wondered what school would be like once the word got out about Sean. She was more worried about the reputation she would get if Sean was called a freak; others might call her a freak also.

This was textbook self-preservation scared. She had to figure out some sort of a plan. If Sean were not around, then maybe others would not connect the two of them as family. *If I can just talk Sean into running away before we even start back to school at this new school, then maybe everything will be okay. This should be easy. Kids run away all the time.* The more Susan drew back from Sean, the easier it was for her to plot against him. *One week till we go to Niagara Falls with Grampy. That's where I'll make him run away*, Susan thought quietly.

Felicia, Oden, and Zimbabwe were meeting together. It was not uncommon for team leaders to discuss strategies among each other. However, anytime anyone was in a meeting with Zimbabwe, the strategy was more like a shell game. You throw out two or three ideas, and hopefully Zimbabwe picks the one you're going to use.

Zimbabwe said, "I love it when Malaywah allows me to play with the humans. I have something special planned for this longitude and latitude." Even though there were several other Milkies at the meeting, Zimbabwe directly addressed Oden and Felicia. "If I see one of your Jumpers there, there will be a storm. If I see both of them there, the sky will open up with tremendous thunder and a snow tornado."

Zimbabwe knew that he controlled the second-most powerful staff, and if he wanted to change the weather, his staff would do it.

Even though he was the one who hid Paul and had him training to become a czar, Malaywah's orders came first. As a caveat, any chance that Zimbabwe had to alter the weather was a treat for him. Nothing gave him more pleasure than watching humans complain about the weather.

Felicia said, "Just because a signal 99 could be called doesn't mean you have to try to kill as many humans as possible. However, I will do everything in my power to protect Paul."

Oden said, "You will need to protect him, because Sean was gifted powers of a Milky, and steering Sean will not be easy. But we are on the same page of orders. I will be doing everything in my power to force Paul away from Sean. Between you and me, we may be able to prevent a signal 99 from even being invoked."

Zimbabwe gave a dead stare and chimed in, "I will do what I need to do with this signal 99, and yes, it will be a moment in human time that they will remember. Before I leave, remember what Malaywah said. Nobody is safe, not even you." He pointed at Oden and Felicia.

Zimbabwe's hands and arms were heavily scarred from decades of using that powerful staff, but it was also clear that he had never developed human feelings over all the decades toward these humans. This was the reason that he is so good at wielding his powerful staff.

Felicia was assigned to watch over Paul, and she recruited Mr. Green from another case to help out Sister Joan. Mr. Green was inserted as a scouting leader many years ago; this was Felicia's ace in her pocket in Montreal. Mr. Green was really good with kids.

Oden was keeping his focus on Sean and keeping him safe.

Zimbabwe was a player without a team. His staff trumped both Oden and Felicia's power together. This was why he always worked alone, not to mention he did not play well with anybody else. Zimbabwe has always been unpredictable but someone that Malaywah could always count on.

Felicia arrived to see the setup on the Canadian side of the falls adjacent to the campground where Sister Joan and Mr. Green were setting up camp. Felicia figured with Mr. Green's assistance that everyone would be safe on the Canadian side of the falls.

Mr. Green came to the falls with thirty scouts, and Sister Joan brought thirty kids from the orphanage. Felicia handed Mr. Green his signal 99 jacket, telling him to wear it facing in until he got the word that signal 99 was in play. Mr. Green had never seen a signal 99 jacket.

Felicia said, "I hope we don't have to wear this. Just to remind you, Mr. Green, that the primary objective is to prevent Paul from coming in contact with Sean. If we have to move Paul out of the area or keep him at the camp, then that is what we must do." Felicia continued, "Zimbabwe could drop down any time. Keep an eye on Paul. Malaywah will probably watch this entire timeline. Oden figured that he may have the upper hand on keeping Sean safe and preventing the signal 99. After all, Sean has abilities that could come in handy if the time is right. So far that's not a problem because there is no sign of Sean and his family showing up yet."

Mr. Green looked around. "We need to set up our tents in the middle of this parking lot with the manhole cover in the middle of the tent." He told the scouts that heat from the underground would help to keep the inside of the tent warm. "Let's go, everyone, we have to have it up before dark. There's a good chance for heavy snow and ice tomorrow, so we have to do this right, or we will all be going home early."

Each scout paired off with a child from the orphanage. Paul teamed up with Christopher Hudson. Paul and Chris were tying ropes to concrete blocks to hold the shelters up. The shelter was going up quite fast, and Mr. Green was keeping an eye out for any of Oden's team. Mr. Green had no idea as to when or if Sean would show up, but he knew that this was a good area to set up if he needed to evacuate Paul quickly. He could protect him by keeping him in the tent until Sean left the area.

There were also several Eagle Scouts on the trip to teach the younger scouts survival skills. One of the Eagle Scouts said, "Now that we have the exterior shelter built, everybody pack the snow from outside along the walls of the shelter, then put plastic on the ground inside the shelter, but don't put any plastic over the manhole cover." From tent to tent, they all heard a similar speech, and after about five or six small shelters, the speech just went away. The tents were secured to the blocks holding them fairly tight, and then the snowpack around the bottoms finished the tent building.

Paul and Chris both thought the same thing—building a snow fort and having a snowball fight—but Chris kept them on track with Mr. Green's plans. Mr. Green had all the scouts all working like perfectly oiled engines and in no time had the parking lot looking like a mini tent city. The park allowed the scouts one area to be set up for burning a fire. Sister Joan knew that nothing would make this group sleep better than having their bellies full and their spirits full from a nice evening around the campfire.

Felicia was watching from a nearby distance as night fell and everybody settled in for the night. "Everything is going well," she said to herself. The next morning, Mr. Green pulled out one of the largest skillets you could imagine. He was able to cook ten pancakes at the same time. At that rate, it didn't take long to feed this hungry troop. Paul and Chris were talking about the snowball fortresses that the entire troop was going to set up, and Paul came up with an idea.

Paul said, "If we pour water on it, it will turn to ice, and then we can build it bigger."

Chris laughed and said, "You haven't been here before. I was here two years ago, and the mist coming off of the falls will do it without us using any water. Everything is going to turn to ice, anyways."

The whole troop worked well together, and the fortress was growing by the minute. Other people in the area started to notice the fortress and came over to join in. This was clearly an idea that several of the other scouts had thought about. Four of the Eagle Scouts had been to the falls several times and brought their own wheelbarrows and shovels, and they were bringing snow from other areas to make it bigger.

Felicia looked around and noticed all the attention that the ice fortress was getting from other people at the park. She had one thought similar to the feeling when someone poured cold water down your back. A cold chill! She felt the human emotion of fear!

Felicia saw the other kids coming around the fortress, and she realized too late that all the kids wanted to have part of building the fortress. She tried to use as much of her mind power as she could, trying to redirect them—*go build your own fortress*—but there were too many kids. Felicia was sending four kids away and five more would show up. She kept on redirecting kids and looking for any sign of the O'Neill family or Sean.

Mr. Green joined in to help Felicia redirecting the kids, and finally, there were six separate fortresses going up. Maybe the focus on the other snow fortresses would redirect Sean and Paul from meeting, and hopefully everybody would stay alive. Felicia was thinking that with so many fortresses, if Sean did show up here, it would be easier to keep them apart.

Mr. Green kept the kids busy all day and called to all the kids, "Time to make dinner!" He was standing outside of his tent ringing a large triangle. Everybody came running. The older boys had a nice bed of coals in the fire and plenty of firewood.

Ernie was one of the Eagle Scouts and in charge of the cooking; he wanted to make one more grilling spot. He called out for volunteers, "We need blocks or stones to make another grill spot here."

Chris, Paul, and three other pairs ran off to find some, but Paul stopped and started to stare off into nowhere. "Paul!" Chris said but got no answer. Chris said again, "Paul!"

This time, Paul snapped out of it and said with a scared look on his face, "Something bad is going to happen."

Chris said, "Stop playing around. We need to find these rocks, or we don't eat." Paul had never had a premonition about anything before that he could remember, at least not something that scared him so much.

Paul looked at Chris and said, "You don't feel that?"

Chris said, "Yeah, it's called hunger, and I'm hungry. Come on!"

Later that night, while everybody was enjoying the campfire, they all could hear the icebreakers in the water, keeping the water flowing so the boats could still bring guests in front of the waterfall. The subject of going out on the boat ride in front of the falls kept coming up. Mr. Green thought about it for a while and told himself that there has not been any sign of the O'Neill family yet, why not let them have fun, plus Paul will be contained and easy to watch.

Mr. Green announced, "If this site is squared away first thing in the morning, we will go on the boat ride in front of the falls." Everybody was cheering with excitement—everybody, that is, except for Paul. He was still thinking about the premonition he had earlier in the evening.

Oden was talking to his team. "I have been listening to some of the scouts, and they are all talking about taking the boat ride around the falls. There are three boats, and together. they are big enough for all the kids. If one kid goes for a boat ride, then they will all go, including Paul. If we are told that Sean is definitely going to be here, then this is where we need to make our move. If we take Paul out before Sean even arrives here, then Sean will be safe. Felicia will not be expecting us to make a move until Sean arrives. That's how it's going to happen. This is going to have to be timed just right. The boats are large enough to hold seventy people on it. It will pass along the bridge side for only a short period of time. For this to look like an accident to the humans, we will have to make this as dramatic as possible. We will break off the rudder, and it will lose control. Together our team should be able to guide the boat into the falls. The water being so cold, it should sink pretty fast. Be mindful of Zimbabwe, he can come through at any time and screw up our plan. He always makes an entrance." Oden added, "On second thought, this may not work, signal 99 is not in play yet. We just need to keep Sean away."

Grampy and the O'Neill family were just leaving Schaghticoke Hill. "How long of a drive is it to the falls?" Sean said.

"We should be there in a few hours if the weather holds good," said Grampy.

Susan didn't like to sit so close to Sean, especially for such a long time. She was still scared of him, and Sean knew it.

Sean said, "Susan, you want to see a neat trick?"

Susan thought to herself, *What can of childish trick are you going to show me?*

Sean said, "It's not a childish trick."

"Dad," Susan said, "tell Sean to stay out of my head and stop reading my mind."

Jeffrey was trying his best to come to terms with the changes in Sean, then trying to make light of things. Jeffrey said, "A teenage female's head is a scary place. You really don't want to be in there."

Susan was not amused and said, "Boys are the scary ones!"

Zimbabwe had his eyes planted on Niagara Falls. He was working hard on changing the jet stream to accommodate a massive storm. A change like this would give hardly anybody early warning, especially a group of kids in a shelter or a car traveling on the interstate. Zimbabwe continued pulling hard on the jet stream; he had not been allowed to alter the jet stream in almost three years. There was a HEART test given to Kristine DiMarco, and the rule of thirteen had been issued. Zimbabwe had spun up an F3 tornado, killing her and her entire family as well as three Milky guards. Terminating humans didn't bother Zimbabwe at all. By changing the jet stream, Zimbabwe could produce a massive winter thunderstorm capable of producing tornado activity.

Malaywah and other council members were all together at the Crystal Chamber Palace outside of the Sorting Table, watching the three groups. From here, the Council could focus on any Milky activity on earth. Since there was such a good chance that a signal 99 could be implemented, the chamber was a full house. The entire Council knew what was at stake, and this was the kind of meeting that most council members never encountered during their reign. The council members watched as if they were watching a football game from the stands, except everybody in the stands was rooting for Oden, Felicia, and Zimbabwe to prevent Sean and Paul from meeting.

Malaywah said, "Those two humans have all of earth to prosper except in the same area. Their fates would've been so much different if it had been brought to our attention at the sorting table that they had made contact and then been followed at that moment. A signal 99 is something I don't like to use. They are both prospective Jumpers who are necessary for the humans."

Malaywah continued by saying, "Sean has already been tried and tested and has been gifted powers. I believe he has an advantage to survive if the signal 99 is used, but neither groups of humans have had to deal with someone by the likes of Zimbabwe as group leader. He has always had the ability to stay nonbiased, a characteristic that is always difficult to balance. But he does what I ask him to do!"

Mr. Green could feel the weather changing. He knew that Zimbabwe had to be working in the area but was sure that Felicia would keep Paul safe. The snow was starting to fall, and because the temperature was just about freezing, the snowflakes were very large. The sky to the west was getting dark with the rare noise of snow thunder echoing throughout the falls. Mr. Green had no idea what Zimbabwe had in mind for the area and continued to gather the kids, keeping an especially close eye on Paul. He said, "This looks like it could be a pretty good snowstorm, but the harbor master will cancel the boat ride if the storm gets too bad. This snowstorm will test a large amount of your scouting skills. There are potentially a lot of merit badges to be had."

The kids were all excited with the possibility of additional merits. Paul and Chris's thoughts of making a giant snow fortress and an ensuing snowball fight where changing. They were now thinking of what extra badges they could earn if the snowstorm was bad enough. Chris said to the other scouts, "If this storm is big enough, it could cause people to get stuck in the snow. We could get them out and bring them to safety." The kids were all excited with the possibility of scoring the difficult but prestigious safety badge.

Paul was not a scout but fell into the camaraderie of being part of a group. He thought to himself, *So this is friendship.* Something he had never imagined.

Felicia noticed that Mr. Green and the other Milkies were not focusing on their main duty. It was supposed to be about Paul and the survival of the prospective Jumper Paul. Instead, Mr. Green and two other Milkies noticed at another snow fort on the other side of the parking lot another Milky walking around with a big 7 on her jacket. That could only be one thing. There was another HEART test for another Jumper fixing to take place. Felicia had that deer-in-the-headlights look on her face.

Oden also noticed the big 7 on the jacket over on the end of the east parking lot. With so many Milkies so close, they all lowered their powers because it was just too much noise. Nobody could telepathically talk to anyone.

Felicia made her way to Mr. Green, "I think that the signal 7 crew needs to know what could be going on over here at any time. Put on your signal 99 jacket." None of the other humans in this area were relevant as far as Felicia was concerned.

Mr. Green announced, "The entire troop will go on the twelve o'clock lunch tour of the falls." He reminded them that the boat left the dock at eleven thirty. Mr. Green had not heard any information about the O'Neill family, so as far as the schedule, nothing has changed and continued scouting events.

Mr. Green had been installed into the Montréal area nearly thirty years ago as a master scout, and because of that amount of time around humans, he developed some emotions and also feelings. He was still trying to make a concerted effort to do everything that the troop had planned on doing and didn't see any reason to change anything because Sean wasn't there yet.

Oden was so busy watching the operations at Paul's camp and the signal 7 crew that he didn't notice that Sean had just arrived at the falls.

Oden said to his team, "Spread out to all three of the boats. Paul is going to be on one of the boats, but we will be on all three. The boats will be stopped at the bottom of the falls for the twelve o'clock lunch, and if we need to do anything, that will be the best time."

Oden's senses started to go crazy! Warning alarms are going off in his head. He stopped and started looking around. Just then, a loud roar of thunder, and the snowflakes started to have a sting to them—the snowflakes had some ice in them. Zimbabwe was getting close! Oden knew that Zimbabwe was in the picture, and he started to flex his power. Zimbabwe would do what he wanted with no plan and no concerns.

Oden felt a little confused. There were too many alarms going off in his head for there to just be…

Wait a minute!

Oden's team had already gone aboard on each of the boats.

"It's Sean!" Oden said.

THE COMMON MAN

Oden felt Sean's presence; he had thought that he was feeling another Milky, but it was Sean. Sean was at the falls now, and Oden's entire team was spread out on all three boats, and with their senses lowered, he will not be able to regroup. Oden was left alone to defend Sean from the two other teams. The main player he really was worried about was Zimbabwe.

Sean was now getting into the area, and Paul was going to be on the boat, and nobody had an idea of what Zimbabwe would do.

Felicia felt the same thing…a different smell…a different Milky pitch.

"Sean! He's here!"

Grampy and all the O'Neills had just arrived at the hotel and gone in to check in. The clerk was being controlled by one of Zimbabwe's guards. Even though Zimbabwe worked alone, he brought a couple of Milkies of his own.

The clerk said, "You all arrived here just in time. They think this storm could be a bad one, which means the view from the boat will be amazing."

Zimbabwe had decided that he wanted to play, and he was trying to force Sean and Paul into meeting to see what would happen, and then destroy them both at the same time—*if* he has to.

The clerk said, "I'm sure you can make it, but the boat tour of the falls leaves at eleven thirty, and with the snow falling and the lights from the falls, the view is spectacular."

Jeffrey said, "We've been traveling all morning, and we will probably try to catch the sights tomorrow."

Susan said, "I want to see the snow falling through the lights over the falls. Please, Dad, can we go?"

One of Zimbabwe's guards was just off to the side and was playing Susan like a puppet. Sean kept looking around—so many voices! He was starting to get dizzy—so many voices, so much noise—because he had not been taught how to use his powers without getting sick.

Grampy said, "Let's get checked in and see how the weather is. I think it might be nice to see also."

Sean and Susan were excited with a sense of solidarity; this was the first time in a couple of months that they really got along. As they were leaving, the clerk said, "If you kids miss the boat ride today, there is a large group of kids on the far side of the parking area staging snow forts for a snowball war. The sign says snowball war starts at six o'clock."

The O'Neills all left for the room with excitement in their minds for a great time. When the lobby was empty, Oden swooped in, hoping to stay close enough to protect them even if there was a chance that Sean detected him.

Felicia and two of her team members showed up at the hotel. Oden was ready.

"Felicia," Oden said, "as usual, Zimbabwe is doing his own thing, except this time he may be breaking the rules."

"I think you may be right," Felicia said. "We both need to be watching out for Zimbabwe."

Mr. Green and all the kids were heading down to the boat ramp as the snow was still falling heavily with large flakes. Mr. Green made sure Paul would be on the same boat that he was on; he was feeling a sense of hesitation, that feeling that somebody was doing more than just watching you. Mr. Green was positive that there would be other guards close by—two, no, four. He could smell four, but one was different. Mr. Green couldn't quite put his finger on it, but the second one was different. The one that he smelled first was a deckhand on the boat. He was the one that was being controlled by Zimbabwe. Mr. Green was not sure who he was detecting. Then Zimbabwe's man definitely detected him. Mr. Green said to himself, "I don't think you have the same plans that I have been given." Mr. Green couldn't shake the other smell. He was sure that it was another Milky guard, but he just didn't understand what the other smell was. Council members were nearly undetectable. That counted out Oden and Felicia, as well as Zimbabwe. The smell that he couldn't identify with was because Sean absorbed the powers of Clinton before Clinton was killed in the explosion.

Zimbabwe's men were on all three boats waiting. They were not on the radar of Mr. Green, but clearly on the radar of Felicia. Felicia just figured out that there was a chance that Oden could make a preemptive strike on Paul in hopes of averting the signal 99. Felicia now decided she needed to get to Mr. Green, except there was one problem. With Sean having Clinton's powers, he put off the same signal as any other Milky, so detecting him would be different because he could be mistaken as another Milky.

Time was ticking away for Paul. The boats were loaded, waiting to shove off. Mr. Green had no idea that he was about to do a battle with the deckhand because one of Zimbabwe's deckhands was stalling the departure. Mr. Green thought that the delay was weather related and had no idea that Sean and his family were now at the hotel. The facts are that the delay was because Zimbabwe was hoping that Sean and his family would board the same boat as Paul and certainly meet each other.

Mr. Green looked and saw a Milky making a straight line for him. He was thinking to himself that a Milky would not attack another Milky, but this was one of Zimbabwe's Milkies. A large swirl of snow blew by, and Mr. Green got tackled. The two tangled on the backside of the boat nearly invisible due to the snow, each one trying to get the upper hand on the other. Their arms were locked like pythons, each one trying to prevent each other from using his weapons. Both had their nails extended. Mr. Green was stabbed in the leg and let out a primal scream. The two of them fell into the water, and the two of continued to struggle in the freezing water.

The boat whistle blew. None of the scouts had even noticed that Mr. Green was now gone. They were so busy watching the snow fall on the front of the boat. Then Mr. Green popped his head up from the water in excruciating pain. Mr. Green stretched his arm out for an edge of the boat to try to pull himself back onto the boat. Zimbabwe's Milky came up, and the two of them tangled again just as the boat motor started, sucking the two of them into the prop. The two of them were gone! Nobody even noticed. As the bodies continued to churn up the water, the boat's whistle blew again, signaling its departure.

There was a faint "Wait for us, we're coming!" But it was too late; the boat departed. It was Grampy, hollering for the boat.

"I guess we'll do this tomorrow, kids," Grampy said.

Zimbabwe looked down from the clouds and saw the two candidates were close but didn't meet. He decided it was his turn to make a move.

Since he couldn't get them together and see what was going to happen, maybe he could stop the boat and force the one off the boat.

Zimbabwe started running on top of the clouds, churning the clouds faster and faster. The static in the air was starting to create a beautiful light show.

The boat captains were watching the light show as they steered their normal course to the front of the falls. Zimbabwe pulled harder and harder on the jet stream, forcing every stride of power on top of the clouds, making a deafening roar of the wind. The clouds were building thicker as he ran faster.

Zimbabwe was thinking, *Oh yeah, it's party time!*

He was thoroughly enjoying himself. He hadn't had this much fun in a long time. More snow, bigger snowflakes, and the snow was nearly blinding.

The ship captains all received a weather emergency. "Funnel clouds are being spotted to the west of Niagara Falls. All boats return to docks immediately!"

Just then—too late! A funnel showed up on the Niagara River. "Not big enough," Zimbabwe said, as he ran faster. The funnel cloud was nearly touching the water. The boat captains started to change course and headed back to the dock.

Zimbabwe looked down and could see the boats changing course. "No, that's not right…you have to stay together! Time to spread this twister out a little. Let's change this to a Twisted Sister in the water. Twin twisters! Now where do you think you're going?" Zimbabwe was peering down at the water looking for his prize. "There you are, don't worry, I see you," he said to the first tour boat as it was trying to run away from the Twisted Sister. Zimbabwe chuckled to himself and said, "Oh, no, you don't!"

As he pulled hard on the two twisters, trying to control their direction as they wildly spun, he said, "None of you are getting away from me, you're mine. All of you are mine."

One of the tornadoes ripped into the first tour boat. The people were screaming in panic, but there was no mercy on Zimbabwe's part. He didn't care which boat had a Jumper on. He just knew that the gloves were off, and he could make as much carnage as he wanted. Zimbabwe looked at the water, waiting to see if he had gotten his prize from the first boat.

Nothing—next!

He then took the larger of the two twisters and diverted it into another tour boat.

Nothing—next!

"Strike two. You got lucky so far, Jumper."

Now that the collateral damage was out of the way, it was time to get real about devastation. His prize had to be on the other boat. Zimbabwe started running faster on the top of the clouds, making the funnel stronger and bigger and merging the two together. The stronger single twister headed toward Paul's boat. The first two boats and its occupants were spinning in the freezing water. Zimbabwe said, "Get out of my way!"

The boat carrying Paul was turning, the captain was doing everything he could to get out of the way of the twister. "I have you now, Paul!" The twister grabbed the tour boat and ripped it apart. This boat was different than the other two boats. Zimbabwe knew that Paul was on this one.

Heads started to pop up out of the water. Paul and Chris and several others managed to come to the surface for air only to get covered by the waves, gasping for air as another water swell took them under. Paul and Chris were in for the fight of their lives as another swell came, and everybody in the area went underwater again.

There was plenty of debris in the water for the survivors to hold onto but catching one and holding onto it was entirely different task. The storm that seemed to come out of nowhere, the snow, and the cold were taking their toll. The survivors were cold, and hypothermia was settling in fast. Paul and Chris were watching as survivors turned into lifeless floating debris. They weren't but a couple hundred yards from the shoreline, but to them, it looked like miles. Two of the other scouts were on a larger piece of debris and pulled Chris up to it and then Paul. Paul said, "We have to get to shore, or we'll freeze out here."

Zimbabwe said, "Why don't I give you a little push toward the shore, and if you live, hopefully Sean will be nearby." He started to turn the twister around. Just then, a bright bolt of lightning and tremendous thunder followed.

Malaywah had had enough! Malaywah took his staff and struck down Zimbabwe, splitting Zimbabwe and the twister in two.

Malaywah said, "The rules were clear. Zimbabwe broke the rules. I specifically said to do everything possible to prevent the two candidates from coming together, and Zimbabwe intentionally and repeatedly tried to put the two of them together."

Zimbabwe paid the ultimate price for betrayal.

Malaywah said, "Now I need a new council member to take the responsibilities of the weather shifter."

The council members peered down from the Crystal Chamber. Until now, most members had only heard stories about Malaywah using the powers of the staff, but now they've seen the staff in action.

Zimbabwe didn't just get vaporized. Malaywah obliterated him with one powerful strike of his staff.

The snowstorm had magically ended, and the twister was gone. In its path was chaos. People were clinging onto pieces of debris, and in the freezing cold, a strange sense of quiet. The roar of the twister was gone, and you would think you would hear people crying and screaming, but instead, you heard the soft sounds of people shivering and holding on for dear life.

Sean and his family managed to get to safety before the tornado came anywhere near to them, but out in the water, you could hear people crying for help. The water was full of bodies and debris. To Sean and Susan, this was a surreal moment. Sean's world was traveling in slow motion again. He just wanted somebody to pinch him to show him that this was really happening again. Another near miss for him; not a scratch on him, yet all these people around him and their lives were flipped upside down.

There was a crowd starting to build down by the docks. People were coming around because the twister was gone and now seeing the damage left behind in the water. You couldn't see out into the water because of the snow, but everybody knew there were people out in the water. None of the three tour boats returned. The ticket office said there were one hundred and twenty tickets sold for the three boats, plus there were five crew members on each ship.

Rescue boats were quick on the scene but were definitely overwhelmed. There was no way they could pull that many people out of the water in time. There were three rescue boats in operation from the pier that was not damaged. Each boat could only carry six people or 1,600 pounds, safely aboard at a time. They were picking the people that were still moving out of the water, having to do a type of triage, deciding who to bring in their boat. It wasn't fair, but with that many people in the water, they had to grab the strongest first, the ones who seemed like they wanted to live.

Sean was drawn to stay and watch from the pier. The people were being rescued from the water. Each boat came in and quickly unloaded and went back out. There was something pulling at Sean to stay there. Sean couldn't put his finger on it, but he knew there was something or someone in the water that he had to see. Rescue boats continued bringing people in. The people were so cold that all they could do was shiver. Their skin was even too cold to bleed. The cuts just oozed clotted blood. There was no talking or crying, just the sounds of people shivering and teeth chattering. People at the pier were amazed that the tornado popped up seemingly out of nowhere and then just died before it ever came to the shore.

Sean could see another boat coming, and this one drew his attention. The boat had several boys on board. As the boat approached, Sean's body started to shiver, his arms and neck twitching. Sean could feel what someone on the boat was feeling. Sean's lips turned blue as he continued to shake.

Jeffrey said, "Come on, Sean, let's go get warmed up at the hotel, you're shivering."

Sean looked at Jeffrey, trying to talk through his chattering teeth. "On the boat…"

Jeffrey interrupted him in the middle of the sentence and tried to pull him away.

"Wait, Dad. I need to see."

Jeffrey hesitated and watched as the kids were being unloaded from the boat. One by one, the kids were rushed off the boat, and then a mysterious woman with one brown eye and one clear eye grabbed one of the boys and wrapped him completely with a thick robe.

It was Felicia. She tried to rush the boy by, but Sean got a good look at him. The boy's eyes were blue as the ocean.

It was Paul! Sean had an overwhelming sense of déjà vu—you know, the feeling that you get when you know with 100 percent certainty about something. Sean knew this boy, and it was coming to him like a tidal wave.

Felicia was trying to stifle her powers as she got near Sean, but it wasn't working. Felicia could feel a sense of electricity as she got closer to Sean. Sean wasn't shaking anymore; he was drawing power and strength from such a stressful environment and being this close to Felicia. Felicia was starting to weaken as she was focusing her attention on Sean. Paul now was drawing energy from her as well. She rushed by as quickly as she could to get Paul to an ambulance. Sean reached out as she passed by. The three of them felt an electrical current that shorted out the electrical system in the ambulance.

With Clinton's abilities harnessed in Sean, and the power of a powerful council member, Sean jumpstarted Paul's abilities with a simple touch. Felicia now felt the surge of energy that was harnessed in her body returned to her as she was still holding Paul. Felicia put one hand out toward Sean and said telepathically, *Stop…his is not the time. Paul needs time to learn his new abilities. I will explain everything to you and Paul, but we must go.* Felicia then said telepathically, *I know you can hear me. I will send you somebody who will help you learn how to use the electricity inside of you, and you must keep it quiet until you're taught how to use it. It's not just an ability, it is a gift not just for defense but for offense also. This is why you must keep it to yourself until you're taught how to use it.*

Then Felicia grabbed the ambulance and recharged the electrical system, and with a small smile, said, *Sean, you haven't seen anything yet!*

Jeffrey was standing there with a complete dazed look on his face. "Who are you? How do you know about Sean? Tell me something," he said as he stared at Felicia. Jeffrey was staring back and forth from Sean to Paul. Felicia watched them. As if it were magic, the two of them stopped shivering. Felicia and Paul's garments were steaming themselves completely dry. Jeffrey asked again, except this time with terror in his voice. "Who are you?"

Felicia reached out with her left hand and touched Jeffrey on the forehead with her extended index finger. She sent a charge of electricity into Jeffrey to try to give him calm and clarity. "Your son, Sean, has been predetermined as a Jumper. Your lives will change after a major event around his sixteenth birthday. Be supportive of him because he has no idea what is in store for him in the future."

Jeffrey said, "What am I supposed to do? I have one hundred questions and no answers."

Felicia stopped him, "This is not about you. It's about Sean."

Felicia and Paul were leaving in the ambulance. Felicia was thinking about a few things. She was wondering what would have happened if Paul were more conscious when they got so close? Where was the rest of her team? Did Zimbabwe kill them all? Felicia was hoping this was the end for a while and that there would hopefully not be any more close calls, at least until Paul takes his HEART test in three years. Paul pulled his hand out from under the robe and reached up and held on to Felicia's hand, sending an immediate charge to Paul's senses and looking up into Felicia's eyes.

Paul's eyes looked like a child's eyes on Christmas morning opening the present that they have been wanting for such a long time. Felicia knew that she was in trouble and pulled her hand away and stared at this pitiful sight.

Felicia thought to herself, *Now I know why Eileen called you the Misfit Prince! You may be the first Elite Jumper in hundreds of years, and you have a lot of training to do before your HEART test when you turn sixteen. Now that so many of your caretakers are gone, I'll make sure you get back to Eileen myself. You have a long road ahead and a lot to learn in just three years.*

CHAPTER 12

January is supposed to be the purest month of the year—the time of the year that all things are cleansed and covered by snow as a way to sterilize all the bad that is happened over the previous year. As for the Montréal orphanage, it would take many days of blizzards to wash away and sterilize everyone's memory of the past few months.

Paul Washington was back at the orphanage under the care of Sister Joan. The orphanage was not the same since the massive storm that took 105 lives in Buffalo, New York. Sixty-three children lost their lives that day as well as twenty parents or caretakers for the children, eighteen employees of the Niagara Falls tour boat, and four rescue personnel.

Most of the sisters around the orphanage had been doing the best they could over the last month. The main pillar of strength at the orphanage was Sister Joan. She may have survived the storm, but she was not exempt from being shaken. Sister Joan had only known life around the orphanage ever since she was found wandering around the orphanage shortly after World War II. The doctors said she had post-traumatic stress-induced amnesia. This is a long way of saying that she had no idea who she was or where she came from, and this was where she joined the Catholic Church and became a sister.

Malaywah had personally allowed Joan to have her life as a do-over fifty years ago. Joan was a Jumper and had been one of the six women defending an orphanage in Rubenstein, Germany, during WWII. That bravery had been rewarded by being reincarnated as a twenty-year-old woman who would later go on to be a Catholic sister in Canada.

Now after an amazing life full of hundreds of adoptions as a sister, her heart now had a hole in it. That storm claimed sixty-three children from two orphanages in the area. You might as well say sixty-four, because Sister Joan's soul was bleeding every day because of those children; her heart ached for those children.

After a thorough debriefing from the Council, Eileen came to the orphanage to meet with Sister Joan.

Eileen said, "I received a letter from Paul Washington about the tragedy. I know I brought him in as an orphan, but I would like to foster him away from this area so that hopefully he can move on with his life."

Sister Joan had no memory of ever being a Jumper or her former life and could be easily influenced by Eileen's powers, but Eileen didn't need to use them.

Sister Joan said, "That would be great." If Sister Joan were a can of gas, her spirit would be running on fumes.

Eileen took Paul and headed for Virginia Beach, Virginia, to start over again, except this time as a stepmom. Not Zimbabwe's soldier.

Eileen had become very close to Paul. After all, she had already been like a mother to him. After talking with Malaywah, she had decided to try to stifle her abilities completely. She just wanted to get Paul to his HEART test and then figured that she could easily stay quiet as a human. Driving away from the orphanage was like a fresh start for Eileen and Paul. As she crossed the border into New York, she couldn't help but think about the storm that killed so many people. As a Milky, she was not supposed to do any soul-searching. She was just supposed to do whatever it takes to guide her candidate as a Jumper or prevent them from jumping the rest of their lives. Simple, but when you do a lot of soul-searching, simple does not seem so simple.

This has always been the reason why Milkies are not supposed to bond with their human candidates. They end up getting human emotions that mess with their ability to guide their candidate correctly. The way it's supposed to be, not the way the humans want their lives to be.

Malaywah called for a meeting of the entire Council.

The entire Council convened at the great chamber. All council members were required to attend, no exceptions. Council members from around the world all showed up. Malaywah had not had an all-inclusive meeting in nearly three hundred years. This could mean only one thing—there was going to be a vote.

The Council chamber was a packed house. The master at arms was busy checking everyone in assuring that all hands were on deck before Malaywah entered the chamber.

Malaywah stood at the opening, and his presence was announced.

Malaywah called the meeting to order as he came into the chamber, and there was a lot of mumbling and looking. Nobody had ever seen a time when Malaywah had carried the two staffs of power.

Everybody recognized the two staffs. The one in his right hand he carried straight up and down. That was the supreme commander's staff. The other staff was in his left hand, which was nearly equally impressive but also equally as recognizable. It had been Zimbabwe's who had been in charge of the weather currents.

At this time, everybody realized that Zimbabwe was not there.

The story about the storm at Niagara Falls had quickly spread to all Milkies, from the council members to all Milkies around the world. Now they all knew for sure—Zimbabwe was gone.

Malaywah called for silence.

In front of everybody were two marbles, a green one and a black one. Also, there was a piece of parchment.

The master of the arms for the Council announced, "Write down two names, and the two with the most votes will go to the green and black marbles. This vote is for the one who you all want to carry the Weather Staff."

The last time there was an opening for this important spot, Malaywah had made a suggestion, but this time he was silent.

Malaywah gave plenty of time for any and all council members to consult with anyone in the chamber. After a small amount of time, the pieces of parchment were collected, but most of them were blank. Most of members had no desire to be put into that position or nominate somebody for such a high position. Of course, there were a few names, but one of the two highest counts was for Amos, who has spent most of his time overseeing the Korean peninsula. The other name was Felicia, who spent most of her time in Canada.

Malaywah announced that all votes for Amos would be the green marbles and all votes for Felicia would be the black marbles. Both candidates were watching as the master at arms made his way around collecting marbles. The anticipation in the air was electric, causing what appeared as a large, heated lightning display in the sky.

Amos and Felicia sat quietly in front of Malaywah as the master at arms tallied all the marbles.

The master at arms spoke clearly so that the whole Counsel would hear. With just one word, the chamber erupted with celebration.

"Felicia!"

Felicia had seen firsthand the power of the weather staff and did not want it. She didn't have a choice. It was hers now and all the power with carrying it, as well as the responsibility.

Malaywah would now anoint Felicia with a slight touch of the weather staff so that she would never forget the strength and responsibility of such an important staff. With that slight touch, one of her eyes turned in color to black as night and is charged with powers she never could imagine. Now she knows firsthand why people were so scared of Zimbabwe.

The entire Council dispersed into the sorting table and back to their assigned duties on earth, and others continued working around the sorting table until they were needed. Felicia was trying to not forget about her guarantee to Paul. However, she had now been assigned multiple orders with two different Jumpers. She had to assist with a hailstorm in Chile for a signal 13. Next, off to a signal 4 in Brazil with a flash flood. Helping Paul was going to have to wait as she sped off to Chile.

The O'Neill family was having dinner back in Schaghticoke Hill. Ever since Sean's encounter with Paul and Felicia, Sean had been uncharacteristically quiet. That electrical charge from that simple touch had fast forwarded his thought process. This was the kind of electrical charge that the Council endows a Jumper after completing the debriefing after his HEART test. That charge was how a Jumper gets the edge over common people, that something extra, that special gift from the Milkies to assure them that their life was going to be better than a common man. Sean had no idea what this charge he felt was or what he could do with it.

There was a good reason why Malaywah did not give Sean his gift after his HEART test at only twelve years old. Sean had no idea what kind a gift he would need to succeed. The gifts are different for every single Jumper. One Jumper may develop super strength; the next one may get an ability of telekinesis, whereas others just want to be a sports superstar.

This would be Malaywah's dilemma when Sean is retested around his sixteenth birthday because Clint had already gifted Sean with his abilities before he died.

Sean was sitting at the table trying to tune out everything. He was listening like a deaf person with new and powerful hearing aids. Clinton's main ability was that of telekinesis and mental telepathy, and at thirteen years old, Sean was having a very difficult time with it. Sean sat there with his hands on his ears and let out a burst of energy. "Dad, please go to RadioShack and get me some headphones. I can't take listening to everybody's thoughts all day long."

Jeffrey said, "All right, just relax. I'll go and get you some." Just then, Jeffrey was thinking, *Today has been a long day and now my selfish boy wants me to stop everything and go to the store.*

Jeffrey's plate went flying off the table, and Sean stood up with his hands over his ears and yelled, "Selfish! I'll show you selfish!"

Sean was using his powers of telekinesis to throw Jeffrey's plate. Jeffrey stood up with a terrified look on his face. Just like Susan, he, too, was starting to get scared of Sean.

Felicia had wiped Susan's mind clean of the encounter at the falls but allowed Jeffrey to keep a spark of the encounter to calm Jeffrey down. Now Jeffrey thought that somehow the attack at the house that nearly killed his entire family had awakened a part of Sean's brain that normally does not get used, and this was why Sean hears what people are thinking. As for when Sean gets mad, the thing about fire coming out of his hands, well, he did not have an explanation for that.

THE COMMON MAN

Felicia knew that she had had no choice on how she dealt with Jeffery at their meeting at the waterfalls. She knew that Jeffrey was not a Jumper and would probably have a hard time understanding Milky and Jumper cohesion and the Jumper to human cohesion.

Jeffrey bounced out of his chair and quickly decided to try to give Sean some quiet time and took Susan with him to RadioShack.

Sean was sitting on the porch when a voice kept going through his head. It was repeating over and over, "Now is not the time. All will be revealed to you." That's what the lady at the pier had said at Niagara Falls. Sean couldn't get her out of his mind or the boy that she was carrying.

Hearing the voices made him feel like a bird. Like a bird that needed to migrate. He wanted to go home, back to Georgetown, Pennsylvania. It wasn't far away, and he thought that maybe the voices would stop if he was back with his friends.

This was not the first time that Sean had felt like running away; usually, these thoughts came to his head just before a large snowstorm. He had run away four times over the past years and never gotten far. Maybe it was just being young or poor planning or the sense that there was something else in plan for him out there. The last time that he ran away, he thought it was going to be the last time because he almost ruined his relationship with someone that he idolized. He started out running away and stopped at the Mahoney house and sat on the front porch. It was late and the house was dark when he heard someone inside. He looked in the window hoping at was Kimberly, but it wasn't—it was Mr. Mahoney. Sean was pretty sure that Mr. Mahoney heard him out on the porch. He tried to not get caught as he left quickly, but things were never the same ever again. Sean was too embarrassed to talk to Mr. Mahoney, whom he idolized so much, especially since he was so crazy about his daughter. Mr. Mahoney never treated Sean any different, but there was a difference; this ended Sean's trying to leave by running away.

Now, Sean was thinking about running away again. Except Sean couldn't get away from himself. His strange new powers are also strangely like a lonely prison. The voices just would not stop, and he just wanted to be alone. Now a big snowstorm was coming in and that "I've gotta get outta here" feeling just wouldn't go away.

Jeffery had always been a pillar of stability and was just returning from the store. Sean was watching Jeffrey as he hopped out of the car. Sean could see Jeffrey with a big smile on his face.

"I hope this helps," Jeffrey said. Sean put the headphones on and plugged it into his radio. It started playing some music.

Sean gave Jeffrey a big, "Thanks, Dad!"

About a month has gone by, and Jeffrey received a phone call from the sheriff department in Georgetown. It was Chief Lampkin, "Mr. O'Neill, we have someone in custody in regard to the explosion at your house. I know it seems like it's been a while, but these things take time."

Jeffrey said, "Did you catch the guy that got away?"

Chief Lampkin responded, "We will have a lineup of people for your son to identify. Hopefully one of them is the guy, and your son can identify him as the one who ran away."

Jeffery was excited and said, "We will be there in about an hour."

Jeffrey was walking up to Sean to tell him that they had to go for a ride to the sheriff's office, and before Jeffrey could even say anything, Sean said, "Let's go!"

Jeffrey responded, "Sean, you need to stop doing that, at least let me ask the question."

Jeffrey and Sean pulled up to the jailhouse, and Jeffrey said, "There's nothing to be scared of. These guys cannot see you. Just tell the sheriff if any of them look familiar." They went inside and met up with Chief Lampkin, and he assured Sean that they wouldn't be able to see him. The chief took both Sean and Jeffery into a small room with a big window into another room that was brightly lit.

Sean could hear the sounds of cell doors being unlocked, and in walked four guys all of similar build, similar height. The room was brightly lit, and Chief Lampkin was just behind Sean and said, "They not only can't see you, but they also can't hear you either."

The men in the lineup were each holding a number. Sean was staring at number four—it was Mike Bass. He was the accomplice of

James White and was brought in because he was bragging at the bar that he knew what happened at the O'Neill house.

One of the deputies spoke into the microphone and said, "Number one, take one step forward." Nothing, no response from Sean. "Get back in line," the deputy said. "Number two, take one step forward."

Before another second could pass, Sean was staring so hard at number four that Mike started shivering and shaking uncontrollably. Sean was using his powers without even knowing what he was doing. Mike's blood started to boil! A pink froth started to ooze out of his mouth, his body started shaking uncontrollably, and then…Mike defecated all over himself. Sean was cooking Mike from the inside out! Pandemonium in that room broke out. The stench of Mike cooking from the inside out was making the other three men gag and vomit all over the room. Even though they were all in handcuffs, they were all running around screaming, and Mike was screaming even louder as he fell to the floor, uncontrollably shaking. Blood was starting to ooze out of his eyes and ears and now poured out of his nostrils. The other three men from the line up were banging on the door, screaming, "Let us out! Let us out!"

Two deputies opened the door and nearly got trampled by the three men as they ran out the door.

Sheriff Lampkin had ran to that room also; the stench was unbearable. The deputies were trying to control the three men in handcuffs.

Sean continued to stare at Mike as he lay shaking on the floor with fluids extruding from every orifice in his body.

Jeffrey grabbed Sean and pulled him away from the window, turning him away from the gruesome sight inside. Jeffrey didn't know what to do. The smell was cascading throughout the building. All he could do was say, "Oh my god, oh my god."

Still trying to keep Sean from looking into the room, Jeffrey looked at Sean. Sean was sweating profusely. Sean's eyes started to roll in the back of his head, and he started to lose the color in his skin. He was getting lightheaded.

Sean didn't know how to use his powers and was unknowingly expelling so much energy staring at Mike that he was draining the energy out of himself. Sean had developed a weakness, a kind of Achilles' heel, the kryptonite to Superman, or a chink in his armor.

Sean collapsed in Jeffrey's arms. The sweat was pouring off of him like someone had turned on a faucet.

"Help!"

Jeffrey yelled, running out of the room and carrying Sean. The deputies were all scrambling, trying to control the situation in and out of the other room. Now Sean was another casualty.

"Not another one!" the sheriff yelled. "Nobody is to leave the building! Get the rescue people over here in the hazmat suits! I think there's something in the air. Lock the building down."

Nobody had any idea that this was brought on by Sean.

The sheriff was doing what he was trained to do, and that was not to bring anyone else into a hazardous area. The sheriff told rescue the situation that two separate people in two different rooms are unconscious and need medical attention immediately.

It has been nearly a week, and Mike and Sean were still both in a coma. Mike was a vegetable on life support; the only thing that was still alive was his brain, which was hooked up to a machine. The doctors wanted to know what caused this before they turned the machines off. Sean, on the other hand, was put in a medically induced coma to try to get his body back to normal. The doctors could not stop him from shaking and sweating, which was why they put him into a coma. Sean and Mike were both put into isolation in the same room. The doctors were thinking maybe it was a type of virus. But the blood work showed nothing. As for all the others at the jailhouse, they were being kept in isolation at the jailhouse. Several deputies from the nearby town were helping with the day-to-day operations until the fourteen days of isolation were over, and everybody could be released.

Jeffrey was beside himself. He was locked up at the jail also, fearing he was exposed. Jeffery was furious that he could not be with Susan at home or Sean in the hospital.

Jeffrey blurted out, "How much longer we gonna have to stay here?"

The sheriff said, "I want out of here just as bad as you do. I wish the doctors had an answer to what happened to your son or say something like we are not going to catch whatever they have."

Sheriff Lampkin called the hospital, and the doctor said, "There's still no change in either one of their conditions, and also, we still don't know what caused either one of their conditions."

Oden had been observing through a porthole, watching Sean. He knew what was going on and was very concerned with Sean's powers. Now that Sean was in a coma, he thought it would be a good time to consult the Council on what to do with Sean. Clinton had made Sean a very powerful human by gifting him his powers just before he died and then received another charge at the falls. This could be a chance to put him back in check as a normal human. Oden set off to speak with the Council.

Jeffrey said, "Finally, day fourteen. Now I know what it feels like to be a prisoner." The doctor personally came to the jailhouse, opened the door, and said, "You are all free to go. Whatever Sean and Mr. Bass came down with, the rest of you are obviously not been exposed to."

Sheriff Lampkin, Jeffrey, and the doctor all went into the office.

"Doc, do you have some sort of answer for us?" Jeffrey said.

The doctor answered, "We are monitoring both of them closely. We have been thinking that Sean was going to come out of the coma days ago, and it really could be any day. His white blood cells are replicating and then somehow being reabsorbed by other white blood cells. Mr. O'Neill, I need you to come to the hospital so we can draw blood on you, and I need to see if you or your wife has the same."

"Really!" Jeffrey snapped.

Jeffrey, with an angry look in his eye, was trying to hold back his emotions and said, "Maybe you didn't get the memo! My wife was killed. He who speaks before he thinks might end up with a fat lip…Doc!"

Sheriff Lampkin cleared his throat. "What about Mr. Bass?"

The doctor said, "Sorry, Mr. O'Neill, I didn't know."

The doctor looked away and said, "For all purposes, he is brain dead, his signs and symptoms are a medical mystery. He shows signs of being electrocuted, both of his feet and hands likely would have to be amputated if he were to live. All his nerve endings are fried. There is no chance he would have ever come out of the coma." The doctor hesitated. "One thing is for sure, he died a very painful death. It's like he got hit by lightning inside of that room. I'm glad I was not in that room! That charge was so strong that it fried his balls and scrotum completely. That man would not have ever fathered another child…ever! Let alone ever be able to pee again. We would have had to surgically put a permanent catheter in him if he lived, just so he'll be able to pee into a bag."

The sheriff looked at Jeffrey and said, "If that man was the accomplice that got away from your house…I have to say that God made sure that he would never run again, let alone repopulate with that kind of hate in his heart."

Jeffrey responded, "What if that was not the guy? Sean never picked him out. I never saw him at my house."

The sheriff said, "Sean will wake up soon, and maybe he will still be able to identify the man from the lineup."

Oden was meeting up with several members of the Council to figure out what to do with his Jumper, Sean. One council member said, "This Jumper has been tested and passed his test, therefore, we cannot just wipe his mind clean and push the redo button in his brain. He has earned the ability to become a middle-class citizen."

Another councilman said, "He is dangerous, look what he did to that other human, and this is a perfect opportunity to remove him completely."

Another councilman said, "How will we know that he will not do this to another human again? He has the powers of a Milky. These powers were gifted to him, not presented to him after his HEART test like a regular Jumper. He would have to be told how to use his powers for the good of humanity and that he would lose them if you abused them."

Another said, "The powers were a gift, therefore, they should go unchallenged. A gift of powers is a very rare thing."

Oden and all the other council members paused for a minute as the lighting in the crystal chamber brightened. This could only mean one thing. A Power Staff was coming into the chamber. It was Felicia, and as she entered, the lighting in the crystal chamber returned to its normal brightness. In the short time that Felicia had been wielding that staff, her right hand had already developed scars.

Felicia said, "Please continue," as Oden moved from the head of the table.

The Power Staff always made everyone nervous, because it's the power that most council members would love to have, but at the same time, it's the power that nobody wants.

Oden pondered for a moment, trying to weigh the opinions of the other council members, but at the same time, he knew that he was assigned this Jumper and that it was his job to guide him.

Oden thanked everyone for their input, and with that, the meeting was over. They all faded into the floor of the chamber and returned to their assigned duties. Oden and Felicia remained in the chamber.

"What are you going to do?" Felicia said.

Oden stood there with a very perplexed look.

Oden said, "Everybody was correct. Each one of the council members all had correct statements. However, the one that sticks in my mind the most is the question about whether he would do it again to another human. Sean is thirteen years old and does not have the ability to control his emotions and use such a powerful gift in a way that benefits humanity. I know it is quite normal to take away a power from a Jumper when he abuses it…Sean is different! A Milky gave him his powers, as a way to save himself from dying, and I don't know if I can take it away without terminating him. I have never heard of a human possessing the powers of a Milky. To possess a power is normal to guide him on his way, but all that and the ability to terminate a human, plus he can sense our presence, so guiding him is going to be difficult."

Felicia said, "He's a Jumper, and he's your Jumper. It's your call."

Oden responded, "I have already spent so much time with this Jumper. He has been one of the most difficult Jumpers that I have dealt with. I will need your help to suppress his powers until his HEART test where he can be taught and guided with the use of his powers."

Oden looked at Felicia. "You are the one wielding the Power Staff."

Felicia was still new at wielding the Power Staff, but she has done well. This was different. She had to tap this human and not kill him or supercharge his brain that would also kill him. Felicia said, "I will do what you need. I will go and give him a light tap on the bottom of his feet. Time to wake up, Sean. Let's see how you respond."

CHAPTER 13

Eileen was in Virginia Beach as directed by Malaywah and was ready for winter to be over with. The Council had informed her that help was on its way, but no one has shown up yet. Trying to raise a super energetic thirteen-year-old as a single mom in the winter had been very trying. Eileen really wanted to use her powers many times over the past few months because Paul had changed ever since Niagara Falls.

That electrical charge that Paul received from Sean and Felicia healed the frostbite on both of his thumbs. There weren't even any lingering effects, plus it charged him with strength for weeks. The drawback that Eileen had to deal with was the supercharged fighter in him that comes out just aching for blood.

Paul had asked many times about Tran, and Eileen's answer was never enough. Paul wanted some action; he missed the training and fighting. Now with his brain supercharged and an undisclosed ability, plus no support as a Jumper, Eileen had a tough road ahead.

At times, Eileen knew that Paul needed to be able to work energy off without hurting anyone, plus at his age, he needed to be in school around other kids. Paul was enrolled into the local school for the first time in his life and just did not fit in. The other kids were constantly picking on him about the scars on his fingers. They thought that he had some sort of disease, and Eileen intentionally did not enroll him in any sort of gym class because if the kids picked on him about his fingers, then they would be completely ruthless if they saw his feet and the giant claw scar on his back. Eileen could only sit back and wait.

Eileen received word that two Milkies were nearby and could help her with Paul. They were Scott and Sidney Shamrock. They had been assigned in the area as local help for any Milky. They were gym teachers at the gym that was only a block from their house. Scott was given the physique of a well-trained gymnast. His skin was a light bronze and completely ripped muscle. Sydney was only four feet and ten inches tall and could catch the attention of anyone who didn't notice Scott. Eileen was sure that she would have no trouble getting Paul interested in going to that gym.

Eileen said, "Paul, after school today, I want to go and check out the gym. We pass by it almost every day." They walked inside and come to find out a lot of people were interested.

Paul heard one of the older boys say, "Look, guys, it's the freak from school!"

Another boy said, "Look, he's with his mama." The boys all started laughing.

Eileen whispered to herself, "Young humans are the cruelest of creatures." She found herself thinking what Tran would do. She looked at Paul and realized that single motherhood was not going to be easy.

Paul said, "I can take all three of them. Tran trained me well."

Eileen responded quickly, "I thought you might like to work out some energy by working out, not fighting anymore. I don't want you fighting anymore."

Paul responded, "I'm really good at it."

At this time, the three schoolboys had moved on to another area. Eileen had a sigh of relief on her face as Sidney came over and introduced herself. Sidney said, "I mainly teach yoga."

Scott said, "I am the personal trainer and would love to talk, but I have to get ready to start a jujitsu class."

Paul's mind and body language quickly changed. He wanted to run over and get into Scott's class, but at the same time, Sidney had his attention. Eileen knew that she had some help with Paul's focus.

Eileen left Paul in the good hands of Scott and Sidney and went outside. She started to go back to her house when she started to feel the presence of other Milkies. She started to look around. She could feel three…no, four…no, five other Milkies were close by.

One by one, they came out of the gym and came over to her. She was so excited that help with Paul was finally here. Then the reality hit her—they were not here to help Paul. There were three other potential Jumpers here in this area; two of them were fifteen and one was fourteen. Now Malaywah's orders were much clearer. It looked like there was going to be a multiple HEART test with multiple candidates.

Eileen was communicating to the three other Milkies at the gym. Eileen was a new one to them. The others had been watching their Jumpers since birth.

Eileen said, "I am the watcher for Paul Washington."

The next to speak was Theo Denham. Theo said, "I am the watcher of Sylvia, and this is Dawn Denham. She is the watcher of Gail."

Then Terrence Turner chimed in, "I'm Terrence. I'm the watcher of Gisele."

They all continued to communicate for a moment, and something huge stood out. Eileen was the only one who has had any contact with her Jumper. All the rest have just been observing and guiding if necessary, but never actually making contact.

Dawn, Theo, and Terrence had never known a Milky who interacted with their Jumper before their HEART test; normally, the first interaction was a debriefing to teach the new Jumper how to use their gift or enhancement when it was given. Most of the time, there was no interaction at all, especially if no gift is given.

The three of them had so many questions for Eileen. All the questions were similar—what is it like to interact with your Jumper? The questions continued at Eileen like she was in a game of dodge ball and never able to answer any of the questions because it was just one after the other asking questions.

Eileen was trying to answer the first question when a large commotion erupted behind the gym.

Eileen had that sick in her stomach feeling that Paul was in the middle of this.

The four of them ran around the back of the gym. Scott had the problem well in hand...literally. He had Paul on his stomach with one knee in the middle of Paul's neck. Scott had one of the schoolboys that was laughing at Paul earlier pinned to the ground. Scott looked and telepathically told Eileen what happened. Eileen telepathically told Scott that Paul didn't like being laughed at. Scott had just started instructing Paul in his martial arts class and told Paul shoes were not allowed. Paul took off his shoes and socks for the class. That was when the three boys started laughing about his feet.

Paul's feet were large and wide for his size, plus his toes were long and webbed together. Add that to adolescent boys, and you get a fight.

After everyone calmed down, Scott sent all four boys home and was talking to Eileen. "Where did Paul learn to fight like that? He went after those boys so fast, I couldn't get to stop him fast enough!"

Eileen gave Scott some history about Tran training Paul and that was why she brought him to their gym.

Scott said, "His temper is explosive. Sidney and I will work on that."

Eileen asked, "Did Paul draw blood from any of the boys?"

Scott said, with a question mark on his face, "No, I didn't see any blood. What else about Paul are you not telling me?"

Eileen explained as much as she could and was also trying to downplay the potential of Paul's ability. Eileen was trying to take care of her Jumper in a way that no other Milky had experienced, because she was visible and tangible to Paul. For this reason, she was also different.

Scott responded, "Paul hasn't had his HEART test yet, so how can he have an ability? Has he gone through puberty yet?"

Eileen said, "It's complicated! Paul is the one that made contact with Sean O'Neill at the sorting table, and somehow both of them survived the contact. I believe that is what makes him different."

Scott said, "This is that Paul? I've heard of these two humans. They are so rare, you know...survivors."

Eileen said, "Ever since the event in Niagara Falls, he has not shown any signs of this ability. I can only guess that Paul received some sort of short circuit from Felicia when she carried him out of the water. She was a very powerful councilman even before she received the Staff of Power."

Scott said, "I have ten Jumpers, and now four prospective Jumpers, counting Paul, that use this gym. I will talk to the other Jumpers to keep their distance. The three other prospective Jumpers are all girls, and there aren't any coed classes, so they should be safe."

Eileen responded, "I believe that Zimbabwe had his own plans for Paul."

Scott blurted out, "Stories about Zimbabwe get passed around fast, even we heard about Niagara Falls here, heck, I have to hear about everything here!"

Eileen said, "Zimbabwe had Tran training Paul to be a czar, I am sure of it. How else could a human develop powers like absorbing your life force, and I'm sure Tran did this on purpose! Tran kept tormenting Paul over and over, trying to make him lose control. Well, Tran got his wish, and Paul grabbed his leg, and his nails drew blood, and Paul wouldn't let go! Tran lost consciousness and passed out. Only then did Paul let go. If Tran had been a human and not a Milky, I am sure that Paul would have killed the regular human. Tran didn't fully recover from that for over a week."

Scott responded, "Wow! I can only imagine how powerful he will be after his HEART test and when Malaywah grants him even more of an ability. We will all want to be on Paul's good side after the HEART test."

Eileen said, "Tran told me the exact statement. Paul knows that Tran and I are different than other people but doesn't really know how. Paul has known us his entire life, but…he doesn't know who we are or why we are in his life."

Sydney came in on the conversation, "Just listening to you talk about this human, I don't think I could ever raise one as a human. It's easy to steer them in a direction after their HEART test, but to actually live with one of these human children…I can't even imagine. They don't even listen to their parents. One of the Jumpers that I watch over is Nika Heinz. I have watched her since birth and have not had to interact at all. Well, maybe a mental nudge every now and again. Watching you interact with Paul is something I don't want to do as a human."

Sydney shook her head and said, "I wouldn't give up my powers for these humans. That Jumper of yours is going to be hard to control. You need to figure a way to make him less noticeable until after his HEART test. You know what I'm saying…encourage him, but don't forget he is still developing."

Nearly a year had passed, and Eileen's hair had nearly turned completely white, and her ability to use her powers as a Milky was nearly gone from living the lifestyle as a human. She knew that this would happen eventually and accepted her life as a human.

This morning was different. Eileen's memories and powers of ever being a Milky were gone! Paul came into the kitchen for breakfast and started to laugh when he saw Eileen.

"What did you do to your hair?" Paul said. "It's all white."

Eileen was aging and her hair was the first thing that everyone could see.

Eileen responded, "I guess it's time to go get my hair colored." She also laughed. On the way to the beauty shop, she was seeing people that she had known for the past year like they just meet. A Milky could see the difference, but humans could only see a slight change. Humans see the difference as just life and just go on with their life.

Scott and Sydney were looking out the window of the gym and could see Eileen but could not sense her presence as a Milky. They looked at each other and knew that her transformation to a human was complete. They also knew that this would happen, and now when it comes time for the HEART test, she will not know what was happening or be able to interfere with the selection process of whether or not Paul passes or fails the test.

Sydney said, "You realize this means that Paul's HEART test is getting near."

Scott replied, "I believe you're definitely correct. Have you noticed the influx of Milkies in the area over the past few months?"

Sydney said, "There are so many prospective Jumpers in the area that something big is going to happen soon, just like the signal 50 that took place in Shanghai, China." Sydney continued, "That signal 50 handled nearly seven hundred prospective Jumpers, and there were only ten who were allowed to have their ability enhanced."

Virginia Beach, Virginia, was an area with a lot of Jumpers, and because of the population density, there were a lot of prospective Jumpers also. It was much easier to have one HEART test instead of having multiple prospective Jumpers all test individually. Jumpers that have passed their tests are told during their debriefing that their ability comes with a price. The price was not only to benefit humanity but also if there was a HEART test being given in the area, they will need to assist. The signal will be clearly identifiable to all Jumpers and Milkies in the area.

About another year had gone by, and flyers were sent out all around the Virginia Beach area and posted at most gas stations: "Air show on October 31 at the naval base in Virginia Beach, Virginia. Open to the public. All are welcome. Come show your patriotic pride." At the bottom of the flyers was an insignia that humans couldn't recognize, however, all Milkies and Jumpers knew what it meant. Signal 50, this will be another big HEART test.

Malaywah had passed the word at the last Council meeting; due to the volume of potential Jumpers, there will be large group of HEART tests given, so post the notice all around the area.

"Virginia Beach, Virginia area will be having one HEART test for all potential Jumpers between fourteen and sixteen years of age and within a hundred mile range. That means there should be approximately 375 prospective Jumpers that are eligible. Make sure that all Milkies who are watching a prospective Jumper in the area respond."

Most Jumpers had never seen a HEART test larger than a signal 18, and most Milkies only get to see a HEART test of no more than ten candidates at a time, but this looked like a pattern that will not change any time soon.

Over in Georgetown, Pennsylvania, Jeffrey had his house rebuilt on his property. It was a little smaller but bricked for strength. Jeffrey wanted to sell his property, but it seemed like the whole town pitched in clearing away his destroyed house and helped him build his new one. Thanks to a loving town, Jeffrey's mind suddenly did a complete turnaround. Jeffery was ready to come home, especially since Sean came out of the coma and seemed to want to go to Georgetown. Sean has run away from Schaghticoke Hill not once, but twice in the past year. Jeffrey can't stop thinking about last time that Sean ran away. He found Sean sitting under a tree at their old homestead. That was about a month after he came out of the coma. Jeffrey sat down with him and had a heart-to-heart talk with Sean, telling him that they would move back home but not until the house was ready. Sean had something to say to Jeffrey that shook him to the core.

Felicia may have woken Sean from his coma. However, there were some memories from what he did to Mike. Sean's ability to hear the thoughts of people near him now gave him terrible headaches. Felicia thought that she suspended Sean's abilities, but she didn't. Felicia's staff hadn't touched him long enough to suspend Clinton's gift, but it did tone it down, and when he awoke out of his coma, he remembered what he did to Mike!

Sean started out by saying that he has kept it to himself, but it was eating him up inside. That was why he kept running away.

Jeffrey listened quietly and didn't know what to say as Sean talked about the man that killed his mom and sister.

That he was not sorry for killing that terrible man.

Jeffrey interjected, "You didn't do anything! If that was the man that killed your mom, then it was karma, not you! You were not even close to him." Jeffrey was trying to compartmentalize what Sean was saying, what he felt, and what he could believe.

Somehow, he knew that Sean was telling the truth. He had seen Sean do some crazy things, like melt the glass out of the hospital window with his bare hands!

Now it was time to protect Sean. Jeffrey took everything in and told Sean one word: "Family! Don't tell this to anybody, not the sheriff, not anybody. The story I will tell will be that if that guy was the man that got away, then karma killed him…end of story."

Then he punched Sean in the arm, knocking him to the ground. "No more running away."

Jeffrey was laughing. "You're grounded for running away again! If Grampy asks, I grounded you!"

Sean was not ready for that but read his dad's mind that he was glad that that man was dead. Even though he has some sort of ability that he doesn't understand, his dad loved him.

The entire O'Neill family arrived at their house in Georgetown for the housewarming party and was greeted by several neighbors and friends that they had developed over the years, including Ms. Martha Ruby, the school principal, and Mr. Robert Rose, the school guidance counselor who managed to influence so many people in the rebuilding of the O'Neill house.

Martha looked around and smiled to Robert and telepathically told him, *Sometimes it's really good to have powers of persuasion.*

Robert said, "We need to contact Terrel and let them know that Sean is back in town."

Martha turned around and looked at the house that Clinton and Terrel were renting and smiled, "He's watching right now. Clinton would be happy to see that your hard work of getting Sean back here so that we can continue being in Sean's life was back on track."

Grampy and Sean were the first out of the car. Sean was smiling from ear to ear as he looked around. Zeke and Zach were the first to greet him. Sean stayed close friends with them when he traveled back and forth from Schaghticoke Hill during the rebuild, but this time was different—they were home. Sean asked Zeke, "Where is Kimberly?"

Zeke was ready for that question. "She'll be here." Zeke knew that her new boyfriend made sure that she wouldn't, but Zeke wasn't going to say that.

Susan got out of the car without crutches, and everybody started cheering! This was the first time most of the neighborhood had seen Susan without some sort of aid for walking.

Robert came up to Susan and hugged her. "Now that's how you come home!"

"Way to go, Susan!" Everybody was hollering! Susan was so happy, she was crying. "No crutches!" Susan yelled.

Susan had a nice prosthetic right leg that she was so proud of; the top was pink with a pink shoe. That cheer took Sean's mind off of Kimberly as Jeffrey finally got out of the car. Jeffrey's smile was a long time coming; he actually felt the love from his neighbors. The hate and anger from everything that had happened to his family was healing. Even a deep cut will eventually heal.

Jeffrey was carrying a walking cane for Susan just in case she wanted it. The contractor that rebuilt the house was Duke Branson. Duke made the cane for Susan out of the part of the wall that was lying on her. Of course that was not true, but that was what he told Susan so that she would use it and feel like she was stronger than a crutch.

The celebration carried on without a hitch all day long. Mr. Mahoney was busy on the barbecue grill doing what he did best, which was taking care of the kids. Sean was watching him at the grill and asked, "How come you got stuck doing the cooking?"

Mr. Mahoney responded, "Who said anything about being stuck? Cooking is just like building. Practice and anyone can cook. Just about anything can have it taste great."

Sean was smarter than he looked. He was happy that one of his mentors was close to him again, but also, he was trying to use his abilities to find out where Kimberly was. It wasn't working. Felicia had toned his powers down enough that he couldn't abuse them. Sean still had his powers, but it was like using masking tape to tape a crack on a waterline—the tape works now, but soon it will fail, and God help whoever was there when it fails.

Sean remembered what he could do before the coma, but now trying to do the same things gave him a throbbing headache instead of the results that he wanted.

He missed Kimberly but was very respectful to not ask her dad where she was.

Zeke came over with a hot dog in his hand, calling to Sean, "Come on, we're all going to go throw the football."

Sean's probing was over. He noticed that the harder he tried to get into somebody's head, the worse his head hurt. Throwing a football was a much better idea. The two of them finished their hotdogs and headed over to throw the ball.

The crowd now started to thin out as the afternoon moved on. Martha and Robert went over to Terrel's house to give him a full update.

Martha said, "We should be hearing something pretty soon about Sean's HEART test. I didn't think I'd ever say this, but the atmosphere feels almost like Sean will be a regular Jumper and not a threat."

Robert responded, "The last Jumper that I helped with was pretty easy. It was a pretty good assignment. Her name was Kelsey, and her ability that was given to her was to lead and serve other humans! Of course, she ran for congressman. Her opponent had run unchallenged the last two elections. With her ability, she was able to win the election and is doing quite well in congress."

Martha said, "I'm just wondering what kind of ability Malaywah will bestow Sean, being that he already has Clinton's abilities."

Robert responded, "We will all know real soon. I think what you said earlier will happen. Sean's test is real soon."

CHAPTER 14

Hurricane season was in full force. The tropics had a storm brewing that would be going up the east coast of the United States. Malaywah summoned Felicia to the Council chamber to discuss the storm with her. "I have a signal 13 set to go in effect on October 15 in the Azores. Redirect that storm away from the United States and have it pick up speed and hit the Azores on the 15, and I'm going to lower the signal 13 to a signal 5."

Felicia said, "That's a long pull."

Malaywah responded, "There will be two prospective Jumpers on the main island, so we don't need anything extravagant or with a long duration."

Felicia said, "If you need to take advantage of any more of the storms this season, the Sahara Desert is really active this year, and several storms are blowing off the coast."

Malaywah had a very inquisitive look on his face, and after several moments responded, "I haven't done this in a while, but it sure would speed up the process for the eight HEART tests that are scheduled around October 30 in North America."

Felicia now had an inquisitive look on her face. "What is it that you haven't done in quite a while?" she responded.

Malaywah carefully articulated his thought, "I'm going to line up all eight of the HEART tests so that with one large storm, all eight tests will be in play nearly the same time. I have scheduled a large HEART test in Virginia Beach on the thirty-first, and then I will arrange for the other seven in the area to all be lined up directly behind one after the other. One large storm should handle all eight of the tests."

Felicia said, "To have a storm like that, the first couple of tests are going to be catastrophic."

Malaywah responded quickly, "Actually, you're going to have to keep the storm together for at least two thousand miles. Make the track go from Virginia Beach, Virginia, on a northwest track across the center of Pennsylvania and make a quick turn at Lansing, Michigan, then go over the top of Bangor, Maine."

Felicia responded, "You're going to kill hundreds of humans with a storm like that."

Malaywah had a stern look on his face and grasped his staff tighter with a slight roll with his wrist. Felicia knew not to cross that line, so she redirected her response. "I will enhance a front coming off the Sahara about two weeks prior to October 31. I will use that one." And she faded into the floor of great chamber."

Malaywah went back to work—working on the HEART tests around the world not focusing on any particular human. But he had been watching Sean O'Neill because Sean was gifted with Milky powers. Paul Washington hasn't been his focus point because he had not been informed about his partial ability from Tran.

Halloween was coming, and Eileen was decorating the yard. Paul had finally adjusted to living in Virginia Beach, thanks to a lot of time from Scott at the gym—or should at least that's what Eileen believed. Eileen was just finishing putting some spooky effects on the house when she noticed that Paul wasn't home from the gym. Paul was normally home by five o'clock on Thursday and Friday. Thursday, he was an hour late, and now it's Friday, and he was real late again. Eileen kept looking at her watch. Six thirty…seven…still no Paul.

Mama bear was kicking in; Eileen didn't say anything or at least make a big deal yesterday about being late. She felt something was different—maybe a girl? Maybe. She couldn't guess. She just had to wait for him to come home. Nine thirty, and the door opened. Eileen was waiting for Paul. "Where have you been?"

Paul responded, "I don't want to talk about it." And he went to his room and closed the door.

"That's not going to work!" Eileen sputtered. She went over and opened Paul's door. He had taken his shirt off.

"Really! No knock?" Paul yelled.

Eileen saw the fresh marks on Paul's back and arms. "Fighting again! I thought you were done with that," Eileen said.

Paul responded, "You don't understand! I'm not like other guys. I need to go."

Eileen responded, "Go? What is that supposed to mean? Go where? Where have you been? What's going on with you?"

Paul responded, "Just like I thought, you don't understand, I don't fit in anywhere. I don't look like anyone else, I don't think like anyone else, and I don't belong here. Please just get out of my room."

Eileen tried to say something.

Paul raised his voice. "Please!"

Eileen stepped out and shut the door.

The next morning, Eileen heard on the local radio station, "Hurricane Colleen was stalled near Bermuda and could head toward the east coast." The radio DJ continued, "With only a few days until the air show, most hotels in the area are booked full. So if you live in an area that could flood, you may want to evacuate."

The two DJs were talking back and forth about the storm. Neither of them had experienced a hurricane before. One of the DJs said, "Do you think we will lose power?"

The other responded, "I thought that hurricanes only go to Texas." They laughed back and forth, oblivious to the power of Mother Nature.

After several more hurricane jokes, one of the DJs read the notice that they were told to read, "If you think you live in an area that could flood, you need to leave the area. Local hotels are already fully booked because of the air show, so you're going to have to look for hotels in land."

This was the warning that came across the airwaves.

If the humans only knew.

There was no way for the humans on the east coast to see that Felicia had her heels dug into the storm, spinning it faster and making it more compact so that the storm could make its journey.

THE COMMON MAN

The three television stations and local radio stations didn't have much information about the storm, which would have saved hundreds of visitors who were still coming into the area for the air show—plus the hundreds of Milkies that were directing their Jumpers into the Virginia Beach area for the signal 50.

Not to mention the other seven HEART test sites that were scheduled to be in the path of the storm. Sadly, this was the only warning that came out. The TV was not reporting the damage that was occurring on the island of Bermuda. The TV was just saying that Hurricane Colleen was battering Bermuda.

Eileen went to Paul's door to tell him about the storm. She knocked on the door—no answer. She opened the door, and Paul was gone, and a note was on his bed. "I need to find who I am." That was all it said. She was in panic mode. She ran outside calling Paul's name. She noticed her car was gone. Eileen ran back into the kitchen and opened her purse. Her keys were gone.

Paul had emptied the money jar and taken her car. He was unaware of the storm coming and was heading north. Paul had that weird feeling, like being a bird that knows when it needs to migrate south; however, Paul was being drawn to go northwest.

Paul didn't know where he was going. He was just following something inside himself that said, "Go northwest." Paul didn't have very much driving experience and was constantly taking wrong turns to the east and then to the west. He was determined to go "some place" northwest, and by nightfall, he crossed into Pennsylvania. He stopped to get gas and saw a pay phone. He thought to himself, *Eileen is probably going out of her mind wondering where I went.* So he called home.

No answer.

He thought about calling Scott at the gym but did not know the number.

Eileen, after listening to the news on the radio, was hoping Paul would come home. Some heavy winds and rain had started coming in. The storm wasn't far away.

The news man on the radio said, "Hurricane Colleen is now a major hurricane category five and is now heading on a new course and should impact the entire shoreline of Virginia."

Eileen ran down the street to try to find Sidney or Scott. She was hoping that maybe Paul had said something to them at the gym to the whereabouts that he may have gone. As she came up to the gym, several people were putting boards over the windows in preparation for the storm.

Eileen was out of breath calling for Sidney. "Have you seen Paul?"

Sidney said, "We haven't seen Paul in several days."

Eileen didn't know what to say.

Scott said, "What do you mean? Is Paul missing?"

Eileen responded, "He took my car sometime last night and left a note saying he had to find who he was and left."

Sidney looked at Scott and telepathically said, *He's going to miss his HEART test! He can't miss that test!*

Scott said, "I'll go to the police department and try to get help."

Eileen turned as a large gust of wind blew by. "I'm going to the school. If you see him, tell him to come home."

As soon as Eileen left, Scott told Sidney, "We can't leave the other Jumpers, this storm is part of their test! Paul is going to fail... we have to oversee the others."

Instead of going to a storm shelter, Eileen went home hoping that Paul would come home. The storm was getting closer, and the outer bands of Hurricane Colleen were tearing at the coastline.

Felicia was forcing the pressure even lower in the hurricane, making the storm tighter to make the long trip. Felicia stuck the end of her staff into the center of the storm, grasping the staff and pulling hard, forcing the storm ashore with a twenty-five-foot storm surge, leveling houses and uprooting trees and power poles. People were climbing to the top floors of hotels trying to escape the flood and hurricane force winds.

Malaywah and over three hundred council members were in the Council chamber observing the signal 50 through the chamber's portholes, taking notes on all the different Jumpers in the area and how they were reacting to the situation. Several red lights were lighting up on the chamber floor in front of certain council members, indicating that the Jumper that they were evaluating had been terminated. Malaywah sent a message to the entire Council observing, "Any Milky that has lost their Jumper due to termination is authorized to be absorbed into the human population."

Several of the councilmen looked around to make sure this really came from Malaywah, because he normally called them all back to the sorting table.

Malaywah was turning the portholes of several of the council members as the storm continued on its path to its next targets.

The reports were coming in, and of the 375 Jumpers that were in the Virginia Beach area, only ten showed any signs of selfless compassion to others or bravery in the face of death. Failing a HEART test was very common. Therefore, these individuals, even though they may feel that they should do better in life, would remain as common men and women.

Malaywah looked at the list and saw that Paul Washington was not on the list of those that received a pass. He thought to himself, *That takes care of that problem.*

That could not be any farther from the truth; Paul in fact was being drawn to Georgetown, Pennsylvania, which would be the third of the eight HEART tests that would be given over the next two days.

Hurricane Colleen was having a lot of trouble keeping its strength because now it has been over land for over twenty-four hours. Felicia was doing her best to keep the storm together, even though it was now down to a strong category two storm and passing over Philadelphia, Pennsylvania. That was the second location for the HEART tests. Felicia was already starting to turn the storm toward Georgetown, Pennsylvania. This storm had been on all three TV channels almost nonstop, showing the devastation on the coast and keeping people up to date in the storm's path.

The local TV channel around Georgetown was telling people that the weakened hurricane Colleen was coming and to prepare for heavy rains and strong winds.

Jeffrey was doing the same thing that the rest of the neighborhood was doing, which was getting ready for the storm. Terrel knew that the storm was coming and that this would be part of Sean's HEART test. Sean was doing well in preparations with his family and his neighbors, when all of a sudden, he stopped and was standing in the pouring rain in the middle of the driveway. Tree limbs were breaking, and debris was flying, but Sean just stood there.

Felicia was up in the clouds still stirring the storm and keeping it together, when a part of her remembered the area she was going over, before she took the position with the Staff of Power. She used to be an overseer for Sean and remembered this was his town that she was going over and knew that this was part of Sean's HEART test. She was not an overseer any longer; she was now one of the most powerful council members with the Staff of Power.

As she was looking down, Sean could feel her presence and smiled.

Felicia went back to focusing on the storm as she had to keep the storm together for another one thousand miles.

Just then, Terrel noticed a large section of debris coming up the street. It was being tossed by the wind, and Sean didn't move. Somehow, it bounced in front of him and then it went over him. Sean quickly ran for the house as his dad yelled for him to get into the house.

Felicia was not showing any favoritism to Sean. The storm continued dumping several inches of rain in the area, and the winds were damaging many structures. Streets had turned into flash-flood rivers as tornados spun by.

The storm had passed, and the damage was clear to see. Power lines were on the ground, as well as broken power poles, with several homes damaged from broken and downed trees.

Jeffrey and Sean came outside and could see a house down the street had a tree uprooted and was lying on the house.

Terrel was logging everything that Sean did and reported to the Council. The councilman that received Terrel's report put up a green light.

Malaywah was looking at the lights for Georgetown. Six green lights and four red lights. Malaywah read the names that received a pass and read Sean O'Neill—pass.

A week after the storm, several council members, including Malaywah, went to debrief the Jumpers after the signal 50 ended.

First stop was to the Jumpers at Virginia Beach to explain what they just went through and the new responsibility that they have for humanity. The ability that Malaywah enlightened the Jumpers varies for each Jumper. Some Jumpers received an enhancement in the ability within them. Others received and got a new enhancement, with an explanation of what some Jumpers had developed and how they will succeed.

The first two test sites went well, and after that, the Council was onto Georgetown.

Just like all other test sites, the Jumpers that passed the HEART test in Georgetown were called together at the water and food distribution site. The overseers for each were there. Sean could feel the energy from so many Milkies in one place. Sean was feeling proud as the debriefing went on, as Malaywah explained how they were chosen to receive abilities, and then watching the first two Jumpers get their ability. Then it was Sean's time. Malaywah touched Sean with the staff on his right shoulder, and his headache was gone. That was the first thing that Sean felt. "No more pain!"

Malaywah said, "You have been carrying your ability ever since you were attacked at your house. Your overseers will teach you how to use this gift."

"Finally!" Sean said to himself. "Something in my life makes sense."

As Malaywah was going to the next Jumper, he said telepathically to Sean, *I hope you really absorb the power you have been gifted.*

Sean thought about everything as Malaywah went on to the next two Jumpers. Terrel said to Sean, "I hope you understand how special you are. I know you think you are just like any other Jumper…you're not! You are the only human that I know who can start fire with your hands. That is a powerful ability."

Sean was still taking in everything as the Council left for the next stop. The entire meeting took about thirty minutes for each Jumper, but to each Jumper, it seemed like an eternity.

Sean said to Terrel, "What do I do now?"

Terrel responded, "Most Jumpers don't start to develop their ability until puberty. You are special. You have been gifted with Milky powers, and now you know how to use them to better this area and help humans around you. This is a gift of historic size."

Sean looked down. "I didn't ask for this! I just want...well, I don't know what I want! Now I know how I killed that man that was trying to kill my family. My family will not have to worry about that again."

Terrel interjects, "You will get everything taken away from you if you use your powers to harm humanity. Don't ever forget the number one rule—don't say any of this to any other human."

"Who's to say what is right and what is wrong?" Sean replied. "Killing that monster was the right thing to do, and I would do it again!"

Terrel tried to silence Sean. "Don't talk like that. You don't want the Council to take your gift away! Think about the good you can do for your town and family. Think about the good you can do for yourself."

Sean started to relax.

Terrel continued, "You can ask us for guidance anytime. You are connected to us, and we are connected to you for your life."

Sean said, "I need to get this water and food to my family. They are going to come looking for me."

Terrel smiled. "What is hours to us is only minutes to humans. That is why everything seems like it is going in slow motion when your powers are being used. Your dad is still listening to the same song on the radio. If you need me, just think of my name. It's that easy."

Sean, his mind full of answers and information, also left the tent with an arm full of food and water and a smile.

Sean woke up the next morning thinking that everything was a dream. He listened to Susan in her room, talking to herself that she didn't want to get up because there was still no power, then hearing his dad outside cooking eggs on the barbeque grill. Sean realized, "No headache!" he said to himself as he grabbed a glass and poured a bottle of water in it and quickly made it start to boil. He put the glass down and looked at his hands. "I can do this."

Just then, Susan came into the kitchen. "Is Dad cooking on the grill? I am starving."

Sean was still getting accustomed to his fully functional powers without restraints. He telepathically told Susan, "Go look for yourself."

She responded, "That's rude."

Sean said, "What are you talking about?"

She said, "I heard you."

Sean apologized, "Sorry, I'm not awake yet. He is cooking eggs on the grill." Sean took the debriefing to heart that he couldn't talk about the Milkies or Jumpers to anyone except other Jumpers or Milkies.

The power was out for the following six days, and finally, it came back on. Jeffrey had cooked as much food as he could because it was going to go bad without a fridge to keep it cold. Sean and Susan went door to door passing hot meals. Susan said several times, "I can't believe this food stays warm so long. We put it on these plates thirty minutes ago."

Sean smiled and jokingly said, "I have hot hands."

They were nearly a mile away from their house, and on their way home, they could see a car in the driveway, but from there, they couldn't tell who it was.

As they walked closer, the car looked like so many other cars in the area that got beat to hell by the storm. It had a big dent in the top that looked like a tree limb hit it with a broken side window and back window. The car just sat there for what seemed like a long time, just waiting for something or someone. Nobody got in or out until they started walking up their own driveway. The door opened slowly and out came a young man, dirty and hungry after a long trip with many detours.

The young man said, "I have come a long way, and I don't know where I'm going or who I'm supposed to see, but I know I'm supposed to be here."

Susan said, "Who are you?"

Before the young man could even answer, Sean said, "I remember you. You were the one being carried by that lady at Niagara Falls."

Paul responded, "I remember you also."

Paul reached out his hand to shake hands with Sean, then they heard a loud, "*No!*"

It was Terrel!

He was running from his house toward Sean and Paul, but it was too late.

Sean reached out his hand, and they shook hands, and the power that was in Sean now energized the partial gift that Tran had given to Paul, causing a small light show in the driveway!

Paul finally knew who he was and what he should become.

A bona fide leader, some sort of a czar in power, but definitely not fighting to make a living. This vision showed that his life was meant to be much more than the one he was living.

The handshake to humans may have been seen as quick, but the power that Paul was charged with was powerful!

Susan stood there dumbfounded and confused, just like any other human who had seen an alien for the first time. "What is happening?"

Sean was controlling Susan, but she had just seen in her eyes a giant bluish-green ball of electricity extrude from Sean into Paul.

Susan was a loss for words—just staring at what could only be considered an alien encounter.

Sean said, "Susan, relax...I will explain to both you and Paul what's going on."

Terrel was trying to use all his persuasion powers to separate them and to isolate Sean. However, there was no way that was going to happen. Sean had full and unrestricted powers of a Milky.

Sean started to talk, but Paul's mind was freshly lit like a Christmas tree.

Paul said, "One of my mentors taught me about the Milkies, and I never really believed him, but I knew that he was different than other people. Tran was like an ancient ninja warrior, and he told me that I will be chosen to receive an incredible ability."

"No! No! No! You two are never supposed to be near each other," Terrel spouted, then raised his two hands as to try to push Paul back into his car.

Tran had somehow foreseen this meeting, because one thing that Tran had instilled into Paul over and over was if someone were to grab him like that, pull them forward, roll backward, and then fling them with your feet over your head as the two of you fall to the ground.

Paul did as he had been trained instinctively.

He grabbed Terrel's arms, and with his newly charged energy, pulled Terrel and then launched him with his feet.

Susan watched under the mind control of Sean and could not utter a word as she watched Terrel's flight over the top of the car.

Finally, Susan said, "Who…what are all of you?" She was looking at Sean, completely unable to make a real sentence. "Who are you?"

Sean responded, "I'm no different than anyone else, however, I've been selected to do better in life than you will ever do."

Susan was squinting her face. "I don't get it. What are you trying to say?"

Terrel started getting up and responded, "None of this is supposed to be revealed. It is strictly forbidden for a Jumper to speak of any of this."

Sean interrupted, "Susan's my sister, and I feel like somehow, Paul is my brother."

Terrel was in pain. He had just been overpowered by a human, a human with Milky-like strength and fighting moves of a Milky.

Terrel quickly telepathically sent out a mayday to all Milkies in the area. "The Jumper Sean O'Neill has made contact with the Paul Washington and is divulging critical information and is being leaked out to the human population."

Sean yelled out to Terrel, "He's calling the Council for help."

Paul had no idea what that meant but didn't hesitate to stop Terrel.

Paul ran over and took his two hands and dug his nails into the temples of Terrel, dropping Terrel to his knees.

Terrel stopped his transmission, but the message was sent out.

Paul was draining the life force from Terrel.

"Stop!" Susan shouted.

Paul, hearing a girl scream, released Terrel.

"None of this makes sense to me," Susan said.

Terrel lay there on the ground, panting for life from having his life force being drained. Paul stood there with blood dripping from his fingernails.

All the commotion in the driveway had gotten the attention of Jeffrey.

Jeffrey came running but had no idea what he was running into.

Terrel tried to speak in his weakened condition, "Your actions are causing a path that is not to be passed. Some things are never supposed to be known about by humans."

Sean said, "In my debriefing from Malaywah himself, I was told to never speak about any of this to humans, but it's too late. Susan couldn't unsee what had just happened."

Sean, using his powers of telepathy, stopped everybody. "We need to all go into the house and get out of sight of anyone else."

Jeffrey started to speak, but Seam telepathically told him and everyone else to do as he asked. "We can talk about everything in the house."

Terrel was in virgin territory. He didn't know what he should do. His life force was very weak, but he has only known life as a Milky.

Terrel said, "Can I go with you also? If it's okay with you, Sean?"

Sean was not accustomed to being in charge but was learning fast. Sean helped Terrel and everyone went into the house.

Jeffrey started, "This is my house and my rules. What the hell is going on!" Pointing at Terrel, he said, "His head is bleeding." And then pointing at Paul, he said, "And who are you?"

Susan stood up. She just wanted to know something, anything.

Sean mentally blocked everybody from talking. Sean stood up and walked to the middle of the room and turned his hands into a circle, and they started to glow! Sean quickly had everyone's attention.

Terrel sat injured on the floor and could only watch as Sean explained his power and how he was gifted it and all about his HEART test.

Paul said, "Why didn't I get a HEART test and get an ability?"

Terrel laughed and said, "You left your test, so you failed, and your mother figure died because you left."

Paul had not been able to get ahold of Eileen since he left. He called several times but figured the power was just out from the storm. Paul stood up and raised his voice, "Eileen is dead? I didn't do that."

Paul was clinching his fists and wanted to attack Terrel.

Terrel said, "The Council has been searching for you." He pointed at Paul.

Jeffrey tried to get a word in but was overpowered by Terrel yelling, "You don't understand what you've done!" He pointed at Sean. "You're going to lose your powers."

"And you," pointing at Paul, "you are nothing."

Jeffrey tried again to talk or at least try to understand what was going on. The only words that would come out of Jeffrey's mouth were "I don't understand."

Terrel was still too weak from Paul's attack to stop Sean from explaining everything to everyone. Sean talked and showed his power in detail for over two human hours. Jeffrey and Susan listened like their lives depended in it, and Paul felt cheated by the life he had lived. Terrel couldn't believe that Sean would ever divulge any of this to other humans. But Terrel knew that his SOS made it through, and help was on the way.

Terrel knew that Sean's actions would not go unpunished and that erasing a human's brain was the normal response, but Terrel couldn't do anything but listen and wait for the Council!

ABOUT THE AUTHOR

P.L. Howd grew up as an invisible boy, the middle child of a small-town family in upstate New York. He had a three-mile bike ride to school—uphill on both ways! That was the way he saw life in the mountains and forged his life to see the next sunrise. Writing is something he didn't know he could do until he thought he would die with a brain tumor and that nobody would know he ever existed because he was invisible to most people. He came to see his life in the eyes of every man and woman, and everybody saw herself and himself in one part or more in his writing and storytelling.